FROM THE NANCY DREW FILES

THE CASE: Nancy tries to find out who wants to knock quarterback Randy Simpson out of action— before the game even begins.

CONTACT: Nancy comes to Emerson to spend homecoming weekend with Ned but soon finds the festivities overshadowed by foul play.

SUSPECTS: Danielle Graves—the cheerleader has vowed to make Randy pay for breaking off their romance.

Zip Williams—Russell University's star quarterback has staked his football career on crushing Emerson, at any cost.

Susannah Carlson—the former student has shown up at homecoming, despite the grudge she bears against Emerson for kicking her out of school.

COMPLICATIONS: The sidelined first-string quarterback is also the head coach's son, and neither seems to believe Nancy when she says the threats against Randy are deadly serious.

Books in The Nancy Drew Files® Series

Available from ARCHWAY Paperbacks

THE NANCY DREW FILES™

Case 63
MIXED SIGNALS

CAROLYN KEENE

AN ARCHWAY PAPERBACK
Published by POCKET BOOKS
New York   London   Toronto   Sydney   Tokyo   Singapore

AN ARCHWAY PAPERBACK *Original*

An Archway Paperback published by
POCKET BOOKS, a division of Simon & Schuster Inc.
1230 Avenue of the Americas, New York, NY 10020

ISBN: 0-671-73067-3

First Archway Paperback printing September 1991

10 9 8 7 6 5 4 3 2 1

Cover art by Tom Galasinski

Printed in the U.S.A.

IL 6+

MIXED SIGNALS

Chapter

One

"THAT BANNER looks terrific!" Nancy Drew said, peering through the windshield of her blue Mustang.

When there was no answer from the passenger seat, Nancy reached over and gently nudged her friend Bess Marvin. "Bess, wake up. You've got to see this."

"What?" Bess mumbled, yawning and straightening up. Her long blond hair was a golden tousle around the collar of her denim jacket. "Are we at Emerson already? I just closed my eyes for a second, and suddenly—" Her eyes widened as she saw the purple-and-orange banner strung above the tree-lined street that led up to the college campus. "Wildcats on the Prowl!" she read aloud. "Hey, there's another one: Emerson Welcomes Its Alumni."

Nancy slowed for the traffic and had time to read a final banner strung from a golden maple to a red-leaved one: Come Home to Emerson.

"Whoever planned this did a great job," Bess commented with admiration. "I'm psyched about homecoming weekend, and I'm not even an alum!"

Nancy's blue eyes sparkled with pride. "Ned's in charge of floats for the parade. He said all the committee heads had worked really hard to do something different this year." Nancy's boyfriend, Ned Nickerson, was a student at Emerson College.

Bess smiled. "Well, those banners definitely make a great first impression. I'm thrilled that Ned invited me to come with you. But I do feel sorry for George. She's going to miss out on all the fun."

"Oh, I don't know about that," Nancy said. "George has been so wrapped up in teaching her class, she may not even notice that we're gone!"

Bess's cousin George Fayne was spending the week teaching a water-safety course back home in River Heights.

"There's the oval," Nancy said, pointing up ahead to an oval-shaped drive surrounded by a cluster of buildings. Some of the structures were modern cubes of steel and glass, while others were old-fashioned ivy-covered stone or brick buildings. "Ned said we're staying in Packard Hall. That's just off the next road on the right."

"I remember that dorm," Bess said as Nancy turned her car onto a narrow road. "It's coed, isn't it?"

"Coed?" Nancy echoed, shooting her friend a teasing glance. "Funny how the important details stick in your head, Bess."

"I can't help it," Bess admitted. "But just because boys live in the dorm doesn't mean I'm going to go boy crazy or anything." Bess crossed her arms, and a mischievous smile lifted the corners of her mouth. "At least not until I've checked out what's happening with Jerry. I can't wait to see him."

"You two really did hit it off during winter carnival," Nancy commented. During a previous visit Bess had gotten to know one of Ned's friends, a football player named Jerry McEntee. "We'll probably run into him at the pep rally tonight. Ned said all the cheerleaders and football players would be there."

Pulling her car into a lot beside a tall brick-and-glass building, Nancy braked to a halt.

"This is it," she announced, opening her car door and getting out. She breathed deeply as she stretched her long, slender frame, letting the crisp breeze ruffle her shoulder-length reddish gold hair.

After Bess had dragged her two suitcases out of the trunk, Nancy led the way to the entrance of

Packard Hall. Inside, the girls gave their names to the student at the reception desk. She checked the guest roster, then handed Nancy two keys.

"You'll be staying on the fifth floor, in Room five-fourteen," the girl said, pointing toward the bank of elevators. "Oh, and here's a schedule and some other stuff for homecoming weekend."

After Nancy took the small pile of papers the girl held out, she and Bess headed for the elevators. On the way to their room, they passed a common area with couches, chairs, and a kitchenette.

Their room, halfway down the hall from the elevator, was actually a suite, with two small bedrooms, a sitting room with two couches and a desk, and a private bathroom. "Not bad," Bess said, once they'd checked it out. "How did Ned manage to get a suite for us?"

"Actually, I think Dean Jarvis arranged it, to thank us for catching the person who stole the empress of Austria's jewels from the museum."

Nancy shivered, remembering how her trip to Emerson's winter carnival had turned into a dangerous chase to catch the thief. Much as she loved a mystery, though, spending time with Ned and Bess was her number-one priority this trip.

Opening one of the pamphlets the girl at the front desk had given her, Nancy said, "There are a million things to do." She skimmed over the list of events. "Today's Thursday. Let's see, there's a pep rally and victory party tonight. Outdoor fair and float parade on Saturday . . ."

While she was reading, someone knocked at the door.

"I'll get it," Bess volunteered, and opened the door.

"And," Nancy continued, still studying her flyer, "there's the formal dance on Saturday night—"

"Which I'd love to escort you to," said a husky voice from the doorway.

The familiar voice made Nancy tingle from head to toe. She turned to see Ned Nickerson, her longtime boyfriend. His six-foot-two-inch frame filled the doorway. An adorable grin lit his handsome face, and his dark eyes sparkled.

"Ned!" Nancy ran into his arms, and he swung her around in a breathless hug. "I thought you couldn't meet us until later," she said, smiling up at him.

"Lab finished early today. Hi, Bess," he said, going over to give her a kiss on the cheek. "I hope you guys are psyched for a great time."

"You bet," Nancy told him. "It'll be good to spend time with you, especially at homecoming." Between Ned's studies and her cases, it was impossible for them to see each other as often as they'd like.

"We're ready to go," Bess piped in. "We can always unpack later."

"Great. You wouldn't mind spending the next few hours rescuing a few desperate Emerson students, would you?" asked Ned. "Some of the parade participants could use a hand finishing their floats."

"You mean we'll get a peek at the floats for Saturday's parade?" Bess asked. When Ned nodded, she grabbed her jacket and headed for the door. "You knew I couldn't refuse a chance for a sneak preview. Help is on the way!" she called out into the hall.

Nancy and Ned laughed and followed Bess. They were standing in front of an elevator when the doors slid open and two suitcases toppled out. A young woman stepped out after the luggage, tugging on a tiny cart with a file cabinet on it. There was a hesitant look on her face as she asked, "Is this the fifth floor?"

"Sure is. Here, let me help you with that," Ned offered, bending to grab the largest of her suitcases.

"Thanks," the woman said with a grateful smile. While Bess held the door open, Nancy helped her with the file cabinet.

"That's a lot for one person to carry," said Ned. "Are you switching rooms?"

The woman shook her head. "I'm not a student," she explained. "I just flew in from Chicago for homecoming. I'm staying with my sister, Tamara Carlson. She's in room five-twelve."

"Then we'll be neighbors," Bess announced as

she and Nancy pushed the cart down the hall. "We're in five-fourteen."

"Are you an alumna of Emerson?" Ned asked.

"Well, I did attend Emerson for two years—two of the worst years of my life, I might add," the woman answered, frowning.

Ned flashed Nancy a look that said he was sorry he had brought up the subject.

"Emerson is not near and dear to my heart," the woman added dryly. "I'm here only to show support for my sister. Tamara's been nominated for homecoming queen, and winning is very important to her."

The group came to a halt in front of room 512. "I know Tamara," said Ned, smiling. "I'm on the homecoming committee, so I've met all the nominees. Tamara's a cheerleader and a member of student council," he explained to Nancy and Bess. "I think she's got a good shot at being elected homecoming queen."

The woman smiled, and her harsh expression softened to one of pride. "It's sweet of you to say that. I didn't mean to be so snippy. Returning to Emerson is bringing back a lot of memories. By the way, I'm Susannah Carlson," she added, extending her hand.

Nancy, Bess, and Ned introduced themselves. "Don't worry about it," Bess said good-naturedly as she shook Susannah's hand. "I'm happy to meet someone with more luggage than me!"

Susannah grimaced at her bags. "I know I should travel lighter," she said, "but I run a mail-order business. I can never seem to go anywhere without my files." She opened the door to her sister's room and started dragging her luggage inside. "You may have heard of my company—Susannah's Spices?"

Bess's face lit up. "Of course! I use your Snappy Cinnamon on my toast."

Susannah seemed pleased. "Well, thanks again. Guess I'll see you around this weekend."

After they left the dorm, Ned led the girls along a tree-lined path that led down a hill opposite the oval. At the foot of the hill a lake sparkled in the late-afternoon sun, reflecting the brilliant fall foliage of the nearby trees.

They headed along the edge of the lake and past the boathouse to a large cedar-sided storage shed. When Ned pulled open the sliding door, they were immediately struck with the sounds of voices, pounding hammers, and rock music. The huge open space was filled with floats in various stages of construction and crowds of students scrambling around them. Nancy could make out a globe of the world, a giant top hat, and a train. Some of the creations, still in the beginning stages, were just chicken wire twisted over wooden frames.

"Wow, this place is really hopping," said Bess, pausing next to Nancy just inside the shed door.

"Will these floats really be ready on time for Saturday's parade?" Nancy asked.

"Sure," Ned replied with a nod. "Some of the best ones are whipped together just hours before the parade."

Just then a petite blond-haired girl came barreling through the shed entrance, jostling Nancy as she went by. Her arms were full of stacks of brightly colored tissue paper.

"Kristin, wait up a sec," Ned called as the girl skirted around Nancy.

She spun around and gazed expectantly at Ned. "What's up?" she asked.

Introducing Nancy and Bess to Kristin Seidel, Ned explained, "They're here to lend a hand."

"And in the nick of time!" Kristin said gratefully. "We're desperate for help with our float for the drill team."

"Hey, Nickerson, get over here!" called a voice from the far side of the shed.

With a shrug, Ned said, "Duty calls. See you later." Giving Nancy a quick kiss, Ned took off.

Five minutes later Nancy and Bess were seated on one corner of a raised wooden platform, stuffing a long strip of chicken wire with squares of folded tissue. Kristin had told them it would be the skirt for their float.

"Hey, look at this, Nan," said Bess. "When you surround pink paper with red and white, it looks like tiny rosebuds."

Nancy studied the colorful pattern. "It's pretty, but we'd better find out what the float's supposed to be before we turn it into a rose garden. Kristin ran off before she told us."

They waved at Kristin, who scrambled over and joined them at the platform. "What a great idea!" Kristin said enthusiastically when Bess showed her the rose pattern. "This will make a perfect skirt for the float. It's going to be a layer cake with a banner that says Wildcats Take the Cake."

"Sounds delicious!" Bess commented.

Nancy was reaching for a sheet of red tissue paper when a petite girl wearing an oversize purple-and-orange Emerson jacket stormed by in front of the platform and caught her attention. The girl paused a few feet away from the platform and gave a defiant toss of her jet black hair. Nancy could see that her green eyes were flooded with tears.

"You've got a lot of nerve!" she shouted.

"Oooh, hot news flash," Kristin whispered to Nancy and Bess. "That's Danielle Graves. She's a cheerleader. I bet she's having a fight with her boyfriend."

"Is that him?" Bess's eyes were riveted on a tall, muscular dark-haired guy wearing jeans and a sweater who seemed to be following Danielle. "He's adorable!"

Kristin nodded. "No kidding. His name's Randy Simpson—he's the Wildcats' new quarterback. He and Danielle are a hot item on campus."

"Danielle," Randy said, catching up with her, "don't get all bent out of shape. I can't help—"

"Don't make any more excuses," Danielle snapped, furious. "Who do you think you are? You can't break up with me and get off scot-free." She jabbed Randy in the chest with her index finger as she snarled, "You'll pay for this, Randy Simpson!"

Chapter

Two

DANIELLE GLARED AT RANDY. After shrugging out of the Emerson jacket she was wearing, she shoved it at him, then pushed him away and stormed out of the shed.

As if suddenly realizing people were watching, Randy raised his head and glanced around nervously before stalking off to join a crowd of guys at a float.

Nancy felt embarrassed that such a personal fight had happened right in front of her and Bess. She felt awful for the couple. "It looks like one of the hottest couples on campus isn't a couple anymore," she observed in a low voice to Kristin.

"I'll say," Kristin agreed, her eyes wide with amazement. "It must feel awful to break up in front of an audience. And on homecoming weekend, too."

"I feel sorry for Danielle," Bess commented as she stuffed a piece of pink paper into the wire mesh. "But she can't force him to go out with her."

"I'm afraid it's not that simple for a girl like Danielle," Kristin explained. "She's very status conscious. I got to know her a little when I tried out for the cheerleading squad. Believe me, she's got a pretty inflated opinion of herself, not to mention a nasty temper. She doesn't get mad—she gets even."

Nancy's gaze shifted to the other side of the shed, where Randy was stirring a bucket of papier-mâché. He was surrounded by other guys wearing Emerson team jackets. Nancy guessed they were football players, too, working on their team's float.

"Have Danielle and Randy been dating long?" she asked, turning back to Kristin.

Kristin shook her head. "Just a few weeks. But they've been a popular couple because Randy's on the team and Danielle's a cheerleader." She sighed, then said, "Listen, I've got to dig up some more recruits. See you later."

The girls spent a couple more hours working on the skirt for the drill team's float. Ned checked on them whenever he wasn't called to one of the other floats.

"It looks great!" he told Nancy and Bess when

the skirt was finished. "You've definitely done your duty here," he added. "Come on. We just have time to grab a burger at the student center before the rally gets under way."

"Great." Bess slid off the platform and pulled on her jacket. "I'm starved."

The three climbed the hill and returned to Packard Hall so Nancy and Bess could put on thick sweaters and gloves. Then they headed for the student center, where they gorged on cheeseburgers and french fries. By the time they left for the rally, Nancy noticed that the wind had risen. A full moon hung low in the sky, casting an orange glow over the campus.

"Brrr," she said, putting up the collar of her jacket.

"It's a good thing we ate all that stuff," Bess commented, zipping her jacket up over her sweater. "We're going to need the calories to stay warm at the rally."

"The wind is brutal up here on the oval," Ned said, "but it should die down once we reach the sports complex."

Nancy cocked her head to one side, listening. "Hey, they've started," she said. "I hear drums!"

When they rounded the gymnasium, Nancy was surprised at the size of the crowd. Hundreds of people filled the parking lot behind the gym. Near the center of the lot a large wooden platform had been constructed, and a podium with a microphone stood at the front edge of it, near a set of stairs. The area in front of the platform was cordoned off, Nancy noticed. A huge bonfire roared in the protected section, several yards from the podium.

Emerson's cheerleaders, up on the platform, were spurring on the crowd, their purple-and-orange skirts swirling as they jumped and cheered. The Emerson mascot, a student in a wildcat costume, skipped around the perimeter of the cheerleaders, waving a purple-and-orange pennant.

"Go, Wildcats, go!" Bess shouted, joining in.

Nancy, Bess, and Ned threaded their way through the crowd until they found a spot near the protected area around the bonfire. From there, they could see the cheerleaders' faces more clearly. Danielle Graves was on one end, her black hair flying out as she moved. Nancy was relieved to see that she was smiling brightly. She seemed to have recovered from her scene with Randy.

"See the dark-skinned girl in front, the one with the short, curly hair?" Ned asked, pointing. Nancy found the tall cheerleader in the front line, then nodded. "That's Tamara Carlson, Susannah's sister."

"One of the finalists for homecoming queen, right?" said Nancy, and Ned nodded.

Nancy clapped along as the cheerleaders finished and ran down the steps, still waving their pom-poms. From its place beside the platform, the band played a rousing song, and the crowd clapped along in time.

A handful of school officials took the platform now, and Nancy recognized the bearlike figure of Dean Jarvis among them. One of the others, a tall, hefty man with slicked-back silver hair, stepped up to the podium.

"Who's that?" she asked Ned. "I don't remember seeing him before."

"He's new. Dale Mitchell, coach of the football team," he told her, clapping along with everyone else.

The coach raised his hands and waited for the noise to die down. "I hate to start off on a negative note, but I'm sure you've all heard the bad news. It's true, our quarterback has been benched for this game."

Several groans rose from the crowd. Nancy nudged Ned and asked, "Randy's benched?"

"No," said Ned, bending to speak into her ear. "Randy's the second-stringer. He's been moved up to play quarterback for this game. The first-string quarterback is Josh Mitchell, the coach's son." Ned gave Nancy a meaningful look before adding, "Josh has been put on academic probation because of his grades."

"No matter what you've heard," Coach Mitchell's amplified voice rang out again, "I'm here to promise you that we haven't given up the fight. On Sunday afternoon we're going to give Russell University a beating they'll never forget!"

"Yeah!" the crowd roared.

"Ladies and gentlemen," the coach shouted above the cheers, "I'm proud to present the members of Emerson's winning football team!"

The cheers rose to a roar as the players, wearing their purple-and-orange jerseys, filed up the wooden stairs at the front of the stage. Their heavy footsteps pounded against the boards, making a rumbling noise that added to the excitement. They stood in a single line that stretched across the back of the platform.

"All right!" Bess shouted. "Let's hear it for the team!"

"I'll start with this week's quarterback," Coach Mitchell announced. "Number nineteen, Randy Simpson—"

A loud cheer erupted as Randy emerged from the group, jogged to the front of the platform, and waved at the crowd.

One by one, the other players ran up and waved as each of their names was announced. Nancy looked up at the sea of color formed by the team jerseys. The orange on the jerseys glowed brightly in the flickering light of the bonfire.

"Number thirty-four, wide receiver Jerry McEntee—" the coach announced.

"Hooray!" Bess shouted, jumping up and down. A tall, slim player sprinted to the front of the platform and saluted the audience. "He's just as adorable as ever," Bess murmured to Nancy.

Nancy had to agree. The wind tossed Jerry's thick, light brown hair, pushing a few wild strands over his forehead, and his smile was warm.

When the entire team had been introduced, the players and speakers filed off the stage, and Dean Jarvis took the podium alone. He made a short speech about Emerson's pride in scholastic and athletic achievement. "Before you head off to the victory party in the gym," the dean concluded, "let's hear one more cheer for our new quarterback, Randy Simpson!"

Randy dashed back up onto the platform and leaned into the microphone. "Thanks!" he said. "I just want you to know that the team appreciates your support, and I promise to do my best to lead the Wildcats to a homecoming victory."

Dean Jarvis patted Randy on the back, then walked down the stairs to leave him in the spotlight alone.

"Ran-dy! Ran-dy!" The students chanted as the band began to play again. The drill team formed a line in front of the platform, behind the bonfire.

"Those outfits are great!" Nancy commented, noticing the purple suede boots and sequined uniforms the drill team wore. They split their line in two, marching off symmetrically. The crowd yelled loudly as Kristin Seidel appeared in between the two lines, twirling a flaming baton.

"That's amazing!" said Bess.

Yellow flames danced around both ends of the stick as she twirled it and lightly tossed it into the air. The crowd gasped, then applauded as she caught it and flung it back up between her legs.

A wide smile covered Kristin's face as she caught the baton, marched backward, stopped just two feet in front of the platform, and threw her baton thirty feet into the night sky. Whistles and cheers filled the air.

As the baton descended a moment later, however, fire leaped from one end of the stick and fell onto the stage. Nancy's mouth dropped open in horror as the flames swept across the tissue paper decorating the front of the platform.

Terror froze on Randy's face as the flames danced at his feet. Before anyone could move, the entire front of the wooden stage was being consumed by fire.

Randy was caught behind a blazing inferno!

Chapter

Three

"RANDY'S IN TROUBLE!" Nancy cried, grabbing Ned's arm. "Come on!" Her pulse was racing as she cut through the crowd to reach the cordoned-off area.

Some people in the audience were still cheering—apparently they couldn't see exactly what was happening. But then more and more screams rang out. Nancy and Ned were just ducking under the rope when everyone started shouting and shrieking in panic.

They raced as close to the burning platform as they dared. At first Nancy couldn't see Randy through the cloud of black smoke that enveloped him, but at last she did spot him.

Coughing and choking from the smoke, Randy

had stumbled back a few steps until he was in the center of the platform. His fists were raised, and he was flailing wildly at the smoke, as if he could beat it back. Flames licked up, almost singeing his jeans. From his erratic movements, Nancy guessed that he had to be in shock.

She gasped as a creaking noise rose from the wooden platform. "It's going to collapse!" she shouted to Ned.

She raced around to the rear of the stage, where the fire hadn't yet spread. "Randy!" she shouted, waving her arms to get his attention. "You have to jump off the back! *Now!*"

The platform was about ten feet high, but Nancy knew the jump wouldn't be a problem for an athlete like Randy—if she could only get him to move. She felt desperate as Randy continued to thrash about like a zombie. "Randy!" she shouted again. "You have to jump!"

All at once Randy seemed to snap out of his daze. Nancy saw his eyes focus on her. A second later he scrambled to the back of the platform and plunged off the edge. As he fell to the ground Nancy reached out to grab his shoulders and ease the impact of the fall. She felt herself being pulled to the pavement beside him.

"He's on fire!" Ned yelled from a few yards away.

Scrambling to her feet, Nancy saw that a small flame rose from Randy's pants. He was crawling along the pavement, still coughing. Without pausing, she whipped off her leather jacket and threw it over his legs. Then she pushed him so that he rolled over and smothered the flame.

"Help me grab him," Nancy called to Ned as soon as she was sure Randy's clothes were no longer burning. "We need to drag him clear of the stage." Working together, they tugged Randy a safe distance away from the roaring flames.

"Look out!" someone shouted. At the same time, a loud crack sounded from the flaming platform.

Nancy raised her head just in time to see the wooden stage shift. The front of it collapsed, sending sparks and flames high into the nighttime sky. Nancy shuddered, imagining what would have happened if Randy had waited a minute longer to jump.

She knelt down next to Randy, who was sitting on the concrete, his head in his hands. Ned was on Randy's other side. Nancy's jacket was on the concrete beside him. She could hear the wail of a siren in the distance as she asked, "Are you okay?"

Randy focused on her, a haunted look in his eyes. "I think so. That was so weird. I've never seen anything catch fire so fast." He shook his head as if to clear away the confusion.

Nancy opened her mouth to agree, but was interrupted when Dean Jarvis rushed over, followed by the coach, who was lugging a heavy fire extinguisher.

"Fire trucks are on the way, and so is an ambulance," said the dean. The coach was already dousing the fire.

The dean leaned down to Randy. "How do you feel?"

"I feel all right," Randy insisted. "I'm all right," he repeated, smiling weakly, "thanks to this girl's quick thinking."

Dean Jarvis smiled as he recognized Nancy. "If it isn't Nancy Drew. I should have known that Emerson's favorite private detective was responsible for saving the day." He gave her an appreciative smile. "Thanks for helping us out—again."

"It's the least I could do," Nancy told him. She was going to thank him for arranging the suite for her and Bess, but the husky dean was already rushing off to greet the fire fighters who were arriving.

Nancy became suddenly aware of the groups of students who were clustered around the parking lot, talking anxiously. She'd been so intent on helping Randy that she'd forgotten all about them. A handful of fire fighters were keeping everyone back from the cordoned-off area, while others used a hose to douse the flames.

"Please move on to the gymnasium for the victory party," Dean Jarvis's amplified voice boomed out. He was speaking through a bullhorn that he'd apparently borrowed from the fire chief.

As the students were dispersing, an ambulance

arrived. Nancy, Bess, and Ned lingered nearby while Randy was checked out. Although the hair on his hands was singed, he had managed to escape without injury.

"You were lucky, kid," Nancy heard one of the medics tell Randy.

"That's for sure," Nancy whispered to her friends. "That platform burst into flame so suddenly, you'd think it was—"

Her words were cut off as Kristin Seidel pushed past her and Ned to make her way over to Randy. Nancy noticed that Kristin had tears in her eyes.

"I'm so sorry!" Kristin said in a trembling voice. "I've done that routine dozens of times, and I've never had any problem."

Although Randy was still shook up, he tried to reassure Kristin. "Hey, I'm okay. Don't worry about it."

Her mind racing, Nancy turned from Kristin to the fire fighters, who were searching through the embers of the platform. In all the excitement she hadn't had time to really consider what had happened. But now that she did, something seemed odd to her.

"It doesn't seem normal for wood to burn so quickly," she murmured to Ned. "I'm going to ask." Leaving her friends, she went over to a fire fighter who was poking at a piece of charred wood with a rake.

"Excuse me," she said, "but isn't it unusual for a wooden platform this large to burn in a matter of minutes?"

The man didn't answer right away. "It's hard to say. Depends on what type of wood it was, whether it was dry—things like that."

"But what about—" Nancy broke off as something shiny in the embers caught her eye. "What's that?" she asked, pointing at the object.

The fire fighter leaned forward and prodded it with the tip of the rake. "It's made of glass." He rolled the object toward him, then picked it up with a gloved hand. "A glass jar," he said thoughtfully, turning it over. "The chief should see this."

He went over to the medical van, where a uniformed fire official stood talking with Dean Jarvis. Curious, Nancy followed him.

"Chief, we found this jar in the embers of the fire," the fire fighter said.

"That—that's mine!" cried a distressed voice from behind them. Nancy turned as Kristin left Randy's side and rushed over to the fire fighter holding the jar. "At least, I think it is. It looks like the jar I keep kerosene in to soak the ends of my baton."

"Did you leave this jar near the stage, young lady?" the chief asked Kristin.

"No!" She shook her head adamantly. "Of course not. I left it over in the bushes near the gym. I had to have it close, but I didn't want to bring it too close to the crowd, especially with the bonfire and all."

The chief frowned. "Are you sure you didn't leave it near the platform?"

"Positive," Kristin told him.

"Could've been that some idiot moved it," the fire chief suggested after a short silence. "But it's more likely that it rolled over here."

"Or someone could have moved the jar accidentally," Nancy said slowly. Still, she couldn't rid herself of a niggling doubt that lingered in her mind.

Shaking her head, she picked up her leather jacket and returned to Ned and Bess.

"There's nothing more to do here," Ned told her, rubbing his hands together. "Let's head over to the victory party."

As they walked to the gym, Nancy told Ned and Bess about the fire chief's ruling on the fire. "They think it was an accident," Nancy explained, "but I'm not satisfied with their conclusion. I'm not blaming Kristin, but how *did* that kerosene get so near the platform?" She shook herself, adding, "On the other hand, it doesn't make sense that someone would try to start a fire on purpose."

"I can see that Detective Drew is onto another case," Bess teased.

"Over my dead body," Ned insisted as he pulled open the gymnasium door. "You have strict orders to kick back and only have fun this weekend."

"Well, there's a mystery *I'd* like solved," said Bess, a teasing glint in her eyes. "Rumor has it that a twenty-foot hero is being served—and I want to find it before it's all eaten!"

The gym was already crowded when they entered. A sound system had been set up, and some students were dancing while others dug into the food that was set up against one wall. A cluster of orange-shirted football players was beside the food tables. One of the guys in the group happened to turn as Ned, Nancy, and Bess walked up.

"Bess! Is that you?" he asked.

"Jerry!" Bess rushed over to give him a quick hug. "It's great to see you. You guys looked terrific at the rally. Are you psyched for Sunday's game?" she asked in an excited rush.

"Hey, McEntee," Ned said in greeting. Nancy smiled and said, "Hi, Jerry. We're coming over to check out the food. How is it?"

"Great," he said, grinning.

The four of them dug into the giant sandwich, then climbed up to an empty row of bleachers to sit and eat.

"This is sensational," Bess commented, taking a bite of her sandwich.

Just then Nancy noticed a good-looking guy striding by. He had slicked-back blond hair and a muscular build.

"McEntee!" the guy called, noticing Jerry in the stands. "What's happening?" He climbed nimbly onto the bleachers to shake Jerry's hand.

Jerry introduced Nancy and Bess. "This is Josh Mitchell, our first-string quarterback." He nudged Josh on the shoulder. "At least he was— and will be again, as soon as he gets his grades up."

"Tell me about it," Josh said, obviously embarrassed. "I wish I could be on the field with you guys on Sunday."

"Me, too," Jerry agreed. He turned to Bess to explain. "The Russell Pirates are our biggest rivals, so Sunday's really important for us. Also, if we win, we might have a shot at the state championship."

"After that fire tonight, it's lucky that Emerson still *has* a team," Nancy put in.

Josh nodded. "That was scary. If Randy got hurt, we wouldn't have a chance of winning."

"The important thing is for you to hit the books, man," Jerry reminded Josh, clapping him on the back.

"I know," said Josh. "I'm working on it. Can you believe I've got two papers due on Monday, right after homecoming? But I'll get them in. There's no way I'm going to stay on academic probation for the whole season."

The conversation returned to football. As Josh explained some of the team's new plays, Nancy became a little bored and began to scan the gym.

An orange-and-purple football jacket caught her eye because it was moving straight toward her. She saw that it was Randy. He had changed into clean jeans and a sweatshirt under the jacket.

Nancy did a double take as he moved closer and she could see his face clearly. His eyes were red and his movements stiff and guarded. Nancy wondered if he was still in shock. His eyes were wide in recognition now, and he continued to head in her direction.

"Hey, Randy!" Jerry called as his friend approached.

"How are you?" asked Josh.

"Fine," he replied curtly. The look in Randy's brown eyes darkened as he turned his attention back to Nancy. "Can I talk to you for a second?"

"Sure," Nancy said. Handing her now-empty plate to Bess, she followed Randy down the bleachers to an uncrowded corner of the gym.

Randy leaned against the wall and shoved his hands into his pockets. "I feel sort of strange telling you this," he began. "I mean, you are a total stranger, but I heard Dean Jarvis say that you're a detective."

Nancy nodded. "That's right." Randy's face was ghostly pale, she noticed, and he couldn't control the shaking of his hands as he rubbed his eyes. "Randy, what's wrong? How can I help?"

Randy shoved one hand into a front pocket of his jacket and pulled out a small square of white paper. "I found this note just now when I went back to the dorm to change. Someone had slipped it under the door of my room."

Curious, Nancy took the square of paper from his hand and carefully unfolded it. She was shocked when she read the message that was typed on it.

WE'RE READY TO PLAY KILL THE QUARTERBACK. LOSE THE HOMECOMING GAME—OR ELSE!

Chapter

Four

I CAN'T BELIEVE I'm being threatened," Randy said, his eyes darting nervously around the gymnasium.

"No wonder you're upset," Nancy said sympathetically.

Randy let out a sigh and raked a hand through his dark hair. "This isn't the first threat I've received, either. Someone's been calling me, late at night, telling me to make sure that Emerson loses the homecoming game—just as it says in the note."

"Phone calls?" Nancy repeated. A single note could have been a prank, but this was a pattern of threats, and that disturbed her. "What did the caller sound like? Did you recognize the voice at all?"

Randy shook his head. "No. It's just a hoarse, muffled whisper. I couldn't even tell if it was a man or a woman. The person always phones after midnight, and the message is always the same—lose Sunday's game."

"How long has this been going on?"

"That note's the first written threat—and it's also the first time anyone's mentioned killing me." Randy looked afraid, and Nancy's heart went out to him. "But I've been getting the calls every night for the past week—ever since I was made first-string quarterback."

Nancy bit her lower lip. "Try to think, Randy. Who could it be? Do many people have your phone number?"

"Just the whole campus," he replied. "There's a directory of students. Anyone could get it."

"I see. But out of all the team members," Nancy went on, frowning, "why would you be targeted specifically?"

"If anyone can throw a game, it's the quarterback," Randy pointed out. "I hope you don't think I'm a wimp. I mean, at first I figured the whole thing was a joke. A few nasty calls were easy enough to ignore . . ." He trailed off, glanced around the gym, then met her eyes directly again.

"Until the fire at the pep rally tonight," she finished for him.

Randy nodded. "When I nearly got burned, I began to add things up. I think that kerosene was dumped on the stage on purpose."

"You may be right," Nancy told him. "Who do you think could be making these threats?" she asked again. "Would anyone be that desperate for Emerson to lose?"

Randy hesitated before saying, "I know it seems obvious, but I think some of the Russell Pirates are behind this. Russell is on the other side of town, and we run into their students all the time. I can tell you that their quarterback, Zip Williams, is a shark. The guy has killer instincts on the field."

"Do any of the Wildcats have a grudge against you?" she asked him, thinking out loud. "Or can you think of a reason why any of them would want Emerson to lose?"

Randy seemed shocked at the suggestion, so Nancy decided to check out that possibility on her own before pursuing it with him. Besides, it didn't seem very likely that any of his teammates would want Emerson to lose.

"Okay. What about the school officials?" she pressed. "Have you mentioned these threats to Coach Mitchell or to any of the deans?"

Randy shifted uneasily. "Not yet," he admitted. "I was afraid they'd take me out of Sunday's game—and there's no way I'm going to pass up my first chance to be starting quarterback. The administration is pretty straight. They refused to bend on Josh's probation, even though it would sew up our chances of winning if he were quarterbacking this weekend. I didn't want them to pull me from the game, too."

"I'll start investigating right away," Nancy assured him. "I hope I'll find out who's behind these threats soon, so you won't have to worry about being benched."

"Thanks, Nancy," Randy said gratefully. "I really appreciate your help."

"But if you're in danger, the administration needs to know about it," she warned him. "If anything else suspicious happens, promise me that you'll report it. And be sure to call me, too. Every bit of information helps."

Randy gave her a quick salute. "You got it."

"Can I hold on to this for safekeeping?" Nancy asked, holding up the note between her thumb and forefinger.

"Sure, anything you want." As they started back toward the bleachers, Randy said, "You know, when I made first-string quarterback, I thought it would be my big break. But it's turning out to be the worst thing that ever happened to me."

Nancy punched his arm lightly and said, "I'm sure we'll get to the bottom of this soon." Then, as Randy wandered off across the gym, she rejoined her friends in the bleachers.

"What was that all about?" Bess asked.

"Where's Jerry?" Nancy asked. She was dying

to tell Bess and Ned about her new case, but she didn't want anyone else to hear about it yet.

"He went to get some punch," Bess replied.

Putting a finger under Nancy's chin, Ned turned her to face him. "Uh-oh. I can tell by that look that something is up, Drew," he said.

Nancy nodded excitedly. "Keep this under wraps, but I promised Randy I'd do a bit of sleuthing for him."

"Another case!" Bess squealed as Ned let out a loud groan.

"Shh!" Nancy gave Bess's knee a nudge. "Let's not announce it to the whole campus," she cautioned. Lowering her voice, she told her friends about the threats Randy had received. "After that fire at the pep rally, he's pretty shaken up," she finished.

"Wow," said Bess, her eyes wide. "I don't blame him. I'd be scared to death!"

"So much for kicking back and relaxing," Ned complained. "I wonder if you'll ever have a visit here that doesn't turn into a major mystery."

Nancy just grinned at her handsome boyfriend. "I guess I'll just have to keep visiting until I do!"

"So where do you begin," Bess asked. "Any suspects?"

"Just the entire Russell football team," said Nancy wryly. Turning to Ned, she asked, "Do you know any of the Pirates?"

Ned shook his head. "Not personally. Their

quarterback is dating one of our cheerleaders, so he hangs around on campus occasionally. He gets a lot of ribbing about dating the opposition, but he seems to take it in stride. His girlfriend is Tamara Carlson, the girl whose sister we met this afternoon."

"Right," Nancy said. "With the crowd tonight, he or anyone from the Pirates might have been able to sneak up undetected and dump that kerosene. I'll have to find a way to meet him. In the meantime, I have a few questions for Danielle Graves. She did threaten Randy this afternoon."

"But why would Danielle want Emerson to lose?" Bess pointed out. "She's a cheerleader."

"That's something I'd like to ask her," Nancy admitted. "I need to find some answers—and soon. The game is only three days away."

She stood up when she noticed Jerry returning with punch. "In the meantime, this is a party— and you haven't asked me to dance yet, Nickerson."

"I haven't had much of a chance, have I?" he said. Grabbing her hand, Ned led her to the dance floor, and for a long time, Nancy forgot everything except how wonderful it felt to be in Ned's arms.

"You're pretty terrific, Nickerson," she said, winding her arms around his neck for a slow song. "It seems like forever since we've spent any time alone together."

Ned's eyes shone as he tenderly brushed a strand of hair from her forehead. "If you're going to be on a case, at least it's here at Emerson, where I can still see you."

Nancy nodded. Sometimes her cases took up so much time that it seemed as if there wasn't a minute left over for her and Ned. But every second she did spend with him, Nancy felt like the luckiest girl in the world.

"You and Jerry danced nearly every song together," Nancy said to Bess in the lobby of Packard Hall. Ned and Jerry had just said good night after walking them home from the gym. "I hope you're planning on asking me to be a bridesmaid at the wedding."

"Nancy!" Bess exclaimed in a shocked tone. Then she giggled. "I did have a lot of fun."

They were halfway across the lobby when Bess noticed a line of vending machines. "I could use a snack." She fished some change out of her pocket. "Want something?"

"No, thanks," Nancy replied, glancing ahead at the elevators. Two cheerleaders were standing there waiting. Nancy started as she recognized the girl with long black hair.

"There's Danielle," she whispered to Bess. "I'm going to ask her a few questions."

As soon as Bess got her candy bar from the machine, she and Nancy joined the other girls.

"You guys were great tonight!" Bess said.

"Thanks," said Danielle, smiling. She shook the pom-poms in her hand, and the purple- and orange-foil ribbons shimmered.

"Too bad about the fire," Nancy commented casually.

"I've never seen anything like that!" the other cheerleader, a tall red-haired girl, exclaimed. Nancy noticed that Danielle merely glanced away and began to tap her foot.

Nancy kept her eyes focused on Danielle as she said, "It's a good thing that Randy Simpson's okay. From what I hear, he's Emerson's only hope of winning on Sunday."

"That's a joke!" Danielle snapped.

An awkward silence fell over them. "Uh, don't you think Randy can lead the team to victory?" Bess finally asked.

Danielle's face became drawn with anger. "I wouldn't count on Randy Simpson for anything!" she said bitterly.

She threw her raven hair back with a defiant toss of the head and added, "Randy Simpson should have been burned—just the way he burned me!"

Chapter

Five

NANCY STARED at the petite cheerleader in surprise. "Don't you care about Sunday's game?"

"Not if that creep gets all the glory," Danielle snapped.

The elevator doors opened just then. The three students inside didn't even have a chance to get out before Danielle barreled in, the foil strands of her pom-poms fluttering.

The red-haired cheerleader gave Nancy and Bess an embarrassed smile as the other students quickly shuffled out and she stepped in. The door slid closed before Nancy and Bess could make it in.

"Talk about touchy!" said Bess.

"That's for sure," Nancy agreed. They waited for another elevator and rode up to their suite. After their long day Nancy and Bess still had to unpack. Nancy was relieved to finally tug on her nightshirt and slippers. Curling up on a chair in the living room, she turned her thoughts to the case.

"After that outburst, Danielle is definitely up there on my list of suspects," she said.

Wearing a nightgown, Bess wandered back into the living room, the candy bar in her hand. Stretching out on the couch, she unwrapped the chocolate-covered bar and took a bite.

"I'm not sure I really think she had anything to do with setting that fire tonight, though. I mean, this is probably just a case of bad romance."

"Danielle and Randy didn't break up until today, so it's not likely she had anything to do with the phone calls," Nancy said. "But maybe it's not a coincidence that the threats suddenly got a lot worse today."

She tapped her chin thoughtfully. "Danielle practically admitted that she'd do anything to get even, even if it means that Emerson loses the big game. She could have set the fire and sent Randy that threatening note."

"There's no limit to how far a scorned boyfriend or girlfriend will go," Bess said dramatically, licking chocolate from her fingers. "A broken heart can make people do strange things."

"I knew I could count on you for the romantic point of view," Nancy said with a laugh.

There were other suspects, too, Nancy reminded herself, remembering Zip Williams and the other Pirates, as well as the guys on Emerson's team. Starting the next day, she was going to check all of them out.

"Wake up, Sleeping Beauty!" Nancy called from the doorway of Bess's room. She was already up and dressed, wearing a thick ivory-colored sweater and a suede skirt in a deep shade of green. She held a paper bag in one hand.

Bess cracked an eye open. "What time is it?" she asked, stretching her arms over her head and yawning. "Did I miss breakfast?"

"It's almost nine. I couldn't wake you before, so I went and had breakfast with Ned."

"Guess I was really tired," Bess said, sitting up in bed. "But now I'm starving!"

"Don't worry," said Nancy, grinning as she held up the paper bag. "I brought you some hot chocolate and turnovers. But you have to promise to hurry. We've got a busy day ahead."

After Bess washed and pulled on a denim skirt and pink sweater, she joined Nancy in the living room of their suite.

While Bess ate, Nancy explained her plans. "I have some more questions for Randy, and I want to try to track down Zip Williams at Russell U."

"What about the homecoming events?" Bess

asked, reaching for a flyer on the table. "I don't want to miss anything."

Putting a hand on Bess's arm, Nancy said, "Ned already gave me the rundown. The homecoming queen and king are announced after lunch. Ned says that it's really no big deal, but I wouldn't mind seeing it. And tonight, there are lots of parties around campus." She checked her watch. "If we leave now, we should be able to work on the case *and* fit in all the homecoming stuff."

"Great," Bess said, polishing off a mouthful of pastry. She took one last sip of cocoa and jumped up to get her jacket. "Okay, I'm done. Where to first?"

"I already called Randy's dorm," said Nancy. "His roommate told me that he spends every morning working out at the sports center. I want to try to catch him before he leaves for a class."

Although Nancy had been inside the sports center on previous visits, she knew that the multistoried building contained dozens of rooms, including an indoor track and pool.

"We'll have to find someone to direct us to the weight room," Nancy said as she and Bess approached the complex.

Inside the main entrance, a security guard directed the girls to the weight-training room, on the first floor, beyond the gymnasium and down a hallway. Pushing through a pair of swinging double doors, Nancy saw that they were at one end of a sizable room. Huge steel Nautilus machines were lined up along the mirrored wall nearest the girls. At the far end was a selection of free weights and barbells.

She was surprised to find the room so deserted. Two guys were taking turns on a bench press in one corner. Randy was sitting at a machine in the center of the room, pushing at a lever with his feet. His gray T-shirt was damp with perspiration.

Randy was so wrapped up in his workout that he didn't notice the girls until they were standing right beside him. "Oh—hi, Nancy," he said, glancing up. Nancy introduced Bess.

"Your roommate told us we'd find you here," Nancy said.

"Yeah." Randy pulled his legs back, grunting as he pumped three more times. Then he stood up and wiped the sweat from his face with a towel.

"I like to spend this hour here," he explained. "The place is packed most of the day, but it's reserved for the players for this one hour in the morning and another hour in the afternoon. There's always a trainer nearby, but he usually leaves me alone to follow my own routine." He slid the towel around his neck and walked to the far end of the room, where the free weights were.

As the girls followed, Bess gestured around the nearly empty room. "Where are the other players?"

"Most of the guys come after practice, but I love it at this time when it's quiet." Randy sat down on a padded bench beside a row of bar-bells.

Sitting on the edge of another bench, Nancy said, "There are a few questions that occurred to me this morning, Randy."

"No problem." Randy lifted a hand to brush his dark, damp hair off his forehead. "Shoot."

"It's about Danielle," Nancy began.

Randy rolled his eyes. "You mean Queen Danielle? I guess you heard we used to date. I never should have gotten hooked up with her."

"She seems to feel the same way about you," Nancy told him. "After you two broke up, we heard her threaten to get even with you. Do you have any idea why she's so angry?"

"Not really," Randy replied. "It's kind of embarrassing to talk about all this." He took a deep breath and let it out slowly. "We only started dating a few weeks ago. I got the feeling that Danielle was more into it than I was. I could tell that she really liked being seen with me—as if I were a trophy or something. But I wasn't sure she really cared about me at all."

"Do you think Danielle would actually try to hurt you?" Nancy asked.

"No way," Randy answered without hesitation. "She talks tough, but underneath she's harmless. Like I told you last night, my best guess is Zip Williams."

No one is harmless when they have a strong motive, Nancy thought to herself. Getting to her feet, she said, "Well, thanks for talking to us, Randy. Bess and I had better go if we're going to make it over to Russell U before lunch." Glancing across the room, she saw that the two other players had just finished their workouts and were leaving.

"Anyway, we should let you get back to your exercises," Bess added. "I know you need to be in shape for Sunday's game."

Randy lay back on the bench and rubbed his eyes wearily. Above him hung a long steel rod with round iron weight disks attached at each end. "I'm not sure a workout is going to do any good at this point," he muttered in a discouraged voice. "Don't get me wrong—there's no way I'll give in to the jerk who's threatening me. But the ironic thing is, I'm not an experienced quarterback. The chances are that the Wildcats will lose, anyway."

"Sometimes games are won from determination and sheer luck," Bess put in.

Randy shot her a grateful smile. "I know. And I'm going to play the best game of my life on Sunday." Gritting his teeth, he reached for the bar above his head and lifted it from its Y-shaped resting place.

"Good," Nancy said. "In the meantime, I'll do my best to get some answers before . . ." Her voice trailed off as she noticed Randy's expres-

45

sion change to one of shock and confusion. The rod above him was wobbling in his hands.

Suddenly the weights on the left side of the barbell slid to the end of the bar, and three of them clattered to the floor. Randy grunted as his arms flexed and shifted crazily. He tried to keep the other weights on that side from falling, but the two remaining disks did drop off, hitting the floor with a heavy metallic ringing.

Nancy realized that the weights on the right side of the barbell were now directly over Randy's head. Before she could even move, those weights started shifting toward the edge of the metal bar.

In another second the heavy iron disks were going to drop off the right side of the rod—and land directly on Randy's head!

Chapter

Six

NANCY LUNGED for the bar. Her hands hit it just as the first weight was about to drop. She shoved with all her strength. A second later the weights dropped off the rod, bouncing off the bench a bare inch from Randy's head and hitting the floor with more metallic ringing.

"Are you all right?" Nancy asked breathlessly, helping Randy up to a sitting position. He still clutched the metal rod, and his face was bright red from exertion.

After taking a few gulps of air, he croaked out, "Yeah, I'm okay. If it weren't for you, those weights would have—I was pressing a hundred pounds!"

"How did that happen?" asked Bess, her voice filled with worry.

Nancy pointed to the steel rod. "Isn't there usually something on the ends of these things to hold the weights in place?"

Randy nodded. "There should be a bolt on each end. I guess I should have checked before I started lifting. But when I saw that the right number of weights were on, I didn't bother checking that the bolts were in place."

"What about those two guys who were here?" said Nancy. "Were they using this?"

"Darrell and Frank?" Randy shook his head. "No. I was here the whole time they were working out, and they stuck with the Nautilus equipment." He gestured to the machines. "Somebody just must have forgotten to put the bolts on."

"Unless it was rigged," Nancy pointed out. "If your attacker knew that you're one of the only people who works out at this time of day, he could have rigged the weights to fall."

"That's awful," Bess said. "Randy could have been killed!"

Meeting Randy's eyes, Nancy said soberly, "I think it's time to tell Coach Mitchell what's going on. But first I want to talk to the trainer on duty here."

It seemed as if Randy were going to protest, but he obviously thought better of it, sighed, and said, "I guess you're right."

Slinging his towel around his neck, Randy got

to his feet and led Nancy and Bess out to the hall. They found the trainer on duty in a small office behind the guard's desk. In his twenties, with freckles and curly brown hair, the trainer was sitting back in the chair, resting his feet on his desk and sipping coffee.

"What's up, Randy?" the trainer asked when he saw them. He swung his feet around and stood up.

Randy introduced Nancy and Bess to the trainer, whose name was Joey Nelson. "Nancy wanted to ask you a few questions, Joey," Randy said.

"Sure. How can I help?" Joey turned to Nancy with a smile.

"It's about the weight room," Nancy began. "Did you happen to notice anyone in there tampering with the free weights?"

Joey's reaction was skeptical. "A bunch of people were in earlier, but just the football team has had access for the past hour. I didn't notice anything unusual."

"Can you tell me who besides Randy was in the weight room today?" Nancy pressed.

"I couldn't possibly," Joey muttered, crossing his arms defensively. "I can't keep track of everyone."

Nancy stifled a sigh of frustration. "Did you check the free weights this morning?" When Joey didn't answer, she asked, "Did you check *any* of the equipment this morning?"

Still no answer.

"What's going on here?" Joey finally asked, staring uncomfortably at first Nancy, then Randy and Bess.

Nancy tried to keep the irritation out of her voice as she told the trainer, "What's going on is that Randy was almost beaned by a hundred pounds of weights."

"Someone took the bolts off but didn't remove the weights," Randy explained.

Joey's face paled. "You okay, Randy?" Randy nodded. "Hey, I'm sorry," Joey went on, turning red. "Guess I should have been sticking closer to the weight room."

"Are you sure you didn't see anything funny or anyone acting suspiciously this morning?" Nancy asked Joey once more. "Or maybe even last night?"

He shook his head. "Nothing."

Nancy thanked him, then turned to Randy. "Now, where's Coach Mitchell's office?"

Randy was silent as he led the girls through the sports center. The coach's office was inside the men's locker room, Randy explained. After he made sure that the locker room was empty, he waved Nancy and Bess inside.

"I feel kind of funny going into a guys' locker room," Bess whispered to Nancy, giggling nervously.

Nancy shrugged, glancing at the empty wooden benches that stood between rows of shiny gray lockers. "Female reporters do it all the time," she said. "At least no one's here at the moment."

Beyond the lockers, Nancy could see into an office that was half glass and half white metal paneling. She peered through the glass in the top half and recognized Coach Mitchell's slicked-back silver hair from the pep rally. She couldn't see his face because he was hunched over, talking into the phone. Apart from the metal desk, the office was furnished with a couple of chairs, two file cabinets, and a shelf filled with awards and trophies.

Randy went over and tapped on the glass window before opening the office door. The coach's gravelly voice floated out to them.

"That's what I said, Kyle, it's all on Sunday's game. Six to ten—" Coach Mitchell broke off abruptly as he turned around to find Randy, Nancy, and Bess in the doorway. He cupped his hand over the receiver and opened his mouth to say something, but then he seemed to think better of it. Putting the phone back to his ear, he said, "I've got to go, Kyle."

A moment later the coach hung up the phone, turned back to them, and got to his feet. "Come on in, Randy—ladies." He was about six feet tall, Nancy guessed, with a beefy build and the beginnings of a pot belly.

They sat down in the chairs the coach indicated, and Randy introduced Nancy and Bess. "Nancy's a detective, and—"

"Oh, really?" Coach Mitchell interrupted, amusement crossing his face. "A real private eye, huh?"

This wasn't the first time Nancy had come across someone who didn't take her seriously. She decided to ignore the comment.

"Nancy's a *modern* private eye," Bess put in. "She's solved tons of cases."

"And I've asked her to help me," Randy said. Leaning forward, Randy told the coach about the threatening phone calls, the note, and the incident in the weight room.

"I know that everyone thought the fire was an accident," Nancy concluded, "but I'm not sure it was. Someone's trying to talk Randy into throwing the game. And since he won't agree to it, they're willing to injure him to keep him out of the lineup."

"Very interesting." The coach sat back down in his chair and folded his arms. His silver hair glimmered under the fluorescent lights as he nodded thoughtfully. "I can see why you're alarmed," he told Randy. "Those threats sound pretty nasty."

Nancy was relieved. At least the coach hadn't laughed them out of the office.

"But I still want to play in Sunday's game," Randy said with force and determination.

"Have any of the other football players received warnings about Sunday's game?" Nancy asked the coach.

Coach Mitchell shook his head. "Not that I know of."

"What about Josh?" asked Bess. "He was quarterback for the first few games of the season, wasn't he?"

The coach waved away the suggestion. "No, that's one thing I know for certain. If anyone had crossed my son, he would have told me, just as Randy has." He shuffled some papers on his desk. "You leave this thing to me. In fact, I'm going to call Dean Jarvis right away. This could be just a prank—but we can't be too careful."

"In the meantime," Randy said, "Nancy has agreed to do some investigating." He seemed relieved that the coach hadn't said anything about pulling him from the game.

"If that's okay with you," Nancy added quickly. It would be a lot easier for her to investigate if she had his permission.

"Of course." The coach winked at her. "It can't hurt to have a lady detective on our side, right?"

His attitude grated on Nancy's nerves, but she didn't indicate how she felt. She just smiled pleasantly at him. Whether or not any coach believed in her detective abilities, she was going to crack this case.

"This will take only a few minutes," Ned told Nancy and Bess. "The homecoming king and queen will have their real moment of glory when they lead the parade tomorrow."

"All hail the king and queen," Jerry joked, pausing to make a courtly bow.

It was early afternoon, and the foursome had just polished off a pizza and sodas for lunch at the student center. Now they were on their way to the oval to wait for the announcement of the homecoming king and queen.

As they climbed the small rise leading up to the oval, Nancy saw several dozen students milling around in front of the stone steps of Ivy Hall, a majestic old brick building on the oval-shaped drive. A guy with a clipboard stood talking to a small cluster of students at the top of the steps.

"Are those the contestants?" Bess asked, pointing to the group on the steps. "Boy, do they look nervous!"

"Happens every year. I think the homecoming committee puts something in their food to make them act that way," Jerry cracked.

"How are the winners chosen?" Nancy asked Ned.

"They're nominated by petition. If you can get two hundred signatures, you're a finalist. The final selection is made by ballot. Each student can cast a vote."

The crowd grew quiet as a trumpet began to play. Looking toward Ivy Hall, Nancy saw that the trumpeter, dressed as a royal page, was standing in the center of the steps. When he finished the piece, he announced: "Hear ye! Hear ye! Make way for Emerson College's new king and queen!"

Nancy clapped as a guy on the homecoming committee took the microphone and introduced all the finalists. Tamara Carlson was the only person Nancy recognized.

"And the winners are—" The student read off two names that Nancy didn't recognize, but she applauded enthusiastically, spurred on by the spirit of the crowd.

On the steps, the king and queen joined hands and took a bow. Then the finalists gathered around to congratulate the winners.

"That concludes the royal ceremony," said the announcer. "See you tomorrow at the float parade!"

"Isn't it romantic?" Bess said as the crowd began to disperse. "Queen for the year—"

"Yeah," Jerry agreed, "but it has its drawbacks. The king has to wear funny purple tights for the parade."

Nancy joined in the laughter. Peering over Bess's shoulder, she could see the finalists descend the steps, and she watched as Tamara Carlson cut through the crowd, joining a guy and girl who stood only a few feet from Nancy and her friends. The attractive guy wore a red-and-white Russell U jacket. When the other girl turned, Nancy saw Tamara's sister, Susannah.

Tamara's pretty, dark-skinned face was

scrunched up with disappointment, Nancy saw. She seemed to be on the verge of tears. Susannah reached out and took her sister by the arm.

"Don't feel bad, Tamara," she said sympathetically. "The other students are crazy not to have voted for you. I told you this school is lousy."

The cute guy nodded grimly. "Emerson stinks!" he said in disgust. "And they're going to lose the homecoming game on Sunday. I guarantee it!"

Chapter

Seven

NANCY'S MOUTH DROPPED OPEN. "Who's that guy in the Russell jacket?" she asked Ned.

"That's Zip Williams, Russell's starting quarterback," Ned said, following Nancy's gaze. "I've never met him personally, but everyone on campus knows who he is. Zip is practically a legend in his own time. They don't call him Zip for nothing. He's all over the field when he plays, and he's tough to stop."

"He also has a motive for hurting Randy," Nancy murmured. "I was hoping to find out a few things from him, like whether he was at last night's rally. He's just saved me a trip to Russell." Giving Ned's arm a quick squeeze, she said, "I'm going over to introduce myself."

Ned nodded, checking his watch. "Okay, but I've got to run. My English class is on the other side of campus."

"And I've got practice," Jerry said apologetically. He turned to Bess. "See you there? I'll look for you in the bleachers."

"Sure," Bess agreed, blushing. "I wouldn't miss it for anything."

As the guys left, Nancy and Bess went over to Susannah, Tamara, and Zip. "Hi, Susannah," Nancy said. "Did you get settled in?"

"Yes, thanks to you and your friends," Susannah replied with a smile. Turning to her sister, she said, "These are the people I was telling you about. Nancy and Bess, isn't it? This is my sister, Tamara, and her boyfriend, Zip Williams."

"Sorry you didn't win," Bess told Tamara, "but it must have been exciting to be a finalist."

Tamara shrugged. "It was okay."

"I've been hearing about *you* ever since I arrived on campus," Nancy told Zip. "People are pretty psyched up about Sunday's game."

A cocky grin spread across Zip's face as he said, "I hate to disappoint all the Wildcats fans, but Emerson doesn't have a chance of winning on Sunday."

"That's a little premature, isn't it?" Nancy asked, raising her eyebrows. "After all, anything can happen."

"That's true." Zip shoved his hands into the

pockets of his Russell jacket. "Let me rephrase that. *Randy Simpson* doesn't stand a chance on Sunday. He's a rookie. Our linebackers will chew him up and spit him out."

When it came to competition, Nancy could see that Zip Williams didn't mince words. Winning obviously meant a lot to him.

"Ooh! Sounds scary," Bess put in. "I can see why they call you a shark on the field."

Tamara's expression lightened a little as she tapped her boyfriend playfully on the head. "Zip may be a shark when he's playing football, but he's a marshmallow when he's with me."

"Don't tell them that!" Zip exclaimed, an expression of mock horror on his face. "You'll ruin my rep."

Despite Zip's arrogance, he had a certain charm. Nancy could see why Tamara liked him. But that didn't mean he wasn't responsible for the threats to Randy.

"Well, after seeing the pep rally here the other night, I think the Wildcats are ready for you," Nancy commented.

"Ha!" Zip scoffed. "Randy practically went up in flames, and that's just what's going to happen to him on Sunday."

Nancy blinked. Zip was talking as if he'd been at the rally himself! "Did you actually see the accident?" she asked him.

Zip shifted uncomfortably, then said, "Yeah. I came to see Tamara cheer." Turning to Tamara and Susannah, he said brusquely, "Don't we have to be someplace?" With a quick goodbye, the threesome walked away.

Turning to Bess, Nancy said in a low voice, "Did you see how weirdly he behaved when I asked him about the pep rally?"

Bess nodded. "And he sure acts as if he would go pretty far to ensure a win for the Pirates—to *guarantee* it, as he said himself." She and Nancy headed toward the football field, on the far side of the sports complex. "Do you think he set that fire?"

"I don't know, but I think I have to find out more about him." Nancy plucked at her ivory-colored sweater as another thought occurred to her. "We'd better keep an eye on Susannah and Tamara, too," she said. "Susannah's certainly got a grudge against Emerson."

"And Tamara is Zip's girl," Bess said, finishing Nancy's thought.

Nancy nodded. "They could be working with him. I have to consider the other guys on the Russell team, and I still haven't checked out any of the Wildcats."

Bess said, "The only Wildcat *I'm* interested in checking out is Jerry McEntee. I'll leave the rest of them to you, Nan."

The girls passed through the gate at the far side of the sports center that led directly to the football field. Nancy could see the Emerson team down at one end of the field, dressed in their scrimmage uniforms.

"There's the drill team," Bess said, pointing to a grassy expanse beyond the playing field, where rows of girls were marching. She climbed halfway up the bleachers and took a seat. Resting her elbows on her knees, she stared intently at the players. "I don't see Jerry."

Nancy scanned the group of players as she sat down next to Bess. "Isn't he number thirty-four?" she said, pointing to a tall guy. Jerry's slender, angular frame stood out among the huskier players. "That's him at the end of the line."

Bess jumped up and waved. "Yes, you're right."

Cupping her chin in her hands, Nancy studied the players closely. Randy had said none of the players had a grudge against him, but she knew he couldn't really be objective about his teammates.

Still, as she watched, Nancy didn't notice any sign of anger or unnecessary roughness toward Randy. Judging by the friendly nudges and pats he received, Randy had a good rapport with his teammates. He played most of the scrimmage, except for defensive plays, when he sat with other players on the bench, wiped his face with a towel, and grabbed drinks from his water bottle.

"Looks like practice is over for the drill team,"

Bess said, dragging Nancy from her thoughts. "Hey, there's Kristin." She waved at the pretty blond majorette, who was passing in front of the bleachers.

"How's the float going?" Bess called.

Kristin glanced up and waved. "It's almost finished," she called back. Tucking her baton under her arm, she jogged up into the stands and sat down next to Bess. "The rose pattern you guys came up with looks terrific."

As Bess chatted with Kristin, Nancy glanced around the stadium. Members of the drill team were now filing out of the stadium, she noticed, while girls in cheerleading uniforms were streaming in. Danielle Graves and Tamara Carlson were among the cheerleaders. Susannah, dressed in jeans and a striped sweater, was with Tamara. The sisters paused near the players' bench to watch a play. Then Tamara dashed off to join the other cheerleaders, leaving Susannah at the edge of the field.

"Rats!" A muffled voice at the foot of the bleachers caught Nancy's attention. The team mascot was struggling furiously with the wildcat costume, twisting at its head.

"It looks like the Emerson Wildcat could use a hand," Nancy said to Bess and Kristin. "I'll be right back."

Climbing down, Nancy hopped onto the field and approached the wildcat. "Do you need help?"

"Please!" came the muffled response. "My zipper is stuck."

Nancy found the problem—a clump of fake fur had caught in the track of the zipper. She managed to work it free, then smoothly opened the zipper so that the student could remove the wildcat head.

"Phew!" said the pretty, red-haired girl who emerged. "I thought I'd never get that thing off. Thanks a lot." The girl tucked the wildcat head under her arm and held out her hand. "By the way, I'm Carrie Broder, alias Emerson Wildcat."

"My name's Nancy Drew. Nice to meet you."

Carrie fluffed her curly red bangs and smiled. "I have to run, but maybe I'll see you at the game."

"I'll be there," Nancy said. As Carrie turned and jogged toward the sports complex, Nancy headed back up the bleachers. She had gone only a few steps when a voice distracted her.

"Can't you bend the rules a little?" someone said below her.

"I'm afraid not. Academic excellence is Emerson's number-one priority."

Both voices sounded familiar. Leaning over the aluminum divider at the edge of the bleachers, she saw Coach Mitchell and Dean Jarvis standing in the walkway between sections of the stadium.

"He'll get his grades up," Coach Mitchell insisted. "Believe me, I've read him the riot act on that. And he's dying to play this one game. What's the harm in letting him play this week?"

He must be talking about Josh, Nancy realized.

Dean Jarvis was shaking his head. "It would set a bad precedent—and it would send mixed signals to the other students. Besides, we have a decent replacement in Randy Simpson. Let's give him a shot." He gave the coach a friendly pat on the back. "Sorry, Dale, but Josh is benched until he gets his grades up."

Nancy's mind was racing as she climbed the rest of the way up the bleachers to join Bess and Kristin. The coach wanted his son to play in Sunday's game. Or maybe Josh himself was desperate to get back onto the team roster. If Randy were injured, perhaps the administration would reconsider and let Josh play. It was a possibility Nancy couldn't ignore. Both the coach and his son seemed to like Randy, Nancy reflected. But she had to add them to her list of suspects.

"What's the matter, you guys?" Nancy asked as she rejoined Bess and Kristin. Both girls were staring glumly at the field. Bess was frowning, and Kristin was shaking her head in disgust.

Without looking at Nancy, Kristin pointed at the players. "Our new quarterback is falling apart."

"But he was doing so well at the beginning of practice." Sitting down, Nancy watched Randy stumble through the next play.

She couldn't believe her eyes. Randy lumbered

clumsily into the huddle and then dragged himself into position on the field. "Come on, Randy," Nancy said under her breath. "Look alive!"

Her eyes were glued to the field as the Wildcats ran the play. The center snapped the ball to Randy, who, instead of passing it, tucked it under his arm and began to run with it. A very odd play, Nancy thought.

But not as odd as the way he was moving, as if he were going in slow motion. Nancy felt very uneasy as she watched him stumble forward, jerking unsteadily with each step. This wasn't the running pattern of someone who was tired, she realized. Something was seriously wrong.

After four or five more unsteady steps, Randy fell—facedown on the grass.

"No one even tackled him," Nancy heard Kristin say in disbelief.

The players clustered around Randy, waiting for him to get up, but Randy continued to lie prone.

He didn't budge.

Chapter

Eight

SOMETHING'S REALLY WRONG!" Nancy shouted, jumping to her feet. "Randy passed out!"

She took off down the bleachers and darted across the field to where the players were circled around Randy, their jerseys a wall of orange.

Coach Mitchell ran in from the sidelines and grabbed a player. "Call an ambulance. Now!" he ordered, and the player went racing off to the locker room.

It wasn't easy for Nancy to push past the crowd of players in their bulky equipment, but she managed to edge close enough to get a look at Randy. The team's medic had turned him over, and Nancy could see that he was at least breathing.

"His pulse is steady but slow," said the medic. "Okay, guys, move back and give him some air."

Relieved, Nancy backed out of the crowd. Randy was still alive, but what had caused his sudden collapse?

She touched a nearby player's shoulder pad, asking, "Do you know what happened?"

The player stripped off his helmet, then shook his head. "Not really. He just passed out."

She questioned a few more players, but they all seemed genuinely confused and concerned about what had happened. If any of them had done something to Randy, they were doing a good job of hiding it. At one point Nancy noticed Coach Mitchell watching her. He nodded his recognition, then turned his attention back to Randy.

As Nancy wandered toward the stands, past the players' bench, the water bottles caught her eye. They were scattered along the bench and in the grass below. Randy had been drinking from one throughout the practice, Nancy remembered.

She went over and picked up one of the bottles. The name Gonzales was printed on the plastic. One at a time she checked the bottles until she found the one labeled Simpson. An ambulance was just pulling onto the field, and Nancy ran toward it, Randy's bottle in her hand. She approached the driver and handed her Randy's water bottle.

"You may want to take this to the hospital and

have it checked out." Nancy nodded toward Randy, who was being lifted onto a stretcher by two attendants. "He was drinking from this all afternoon."

"I'll take it to the lab," the uniformed woman assured Nancy, taking the bottle. A moment later Randy was inside the ambulance and the vehicle was pulling away, its emergency lights flashing.

Nancy turned as Bess appeared at her side, asking, "Is Randy okay?"

"I don't know," Nancy replied truthfully. "We'll have to call the hospital later. But in the meantime—" She paused, seeing a husky figure trudging onto the field. "Oh, good. There's Dean Jarvis."

Nancy hurried over to him. "I saw the ambulance from my office and came right over," the dean of students told her. "Is it true that Randy Simpson passed out?"

"I'm afraid so," Nancy answered. "And I suspect that it wasn't an accident. I've been investigating anonymous threats that Randy's been receiving. Now it seems as if someone's making good on those threats."

The dean nodded brusquely. "I heard that you were working on this."

Nancy quickly told him about Randy's water bottle and how the ambulance attendant had promised to have the liquid analyzed. "In the meantime I'd like to search for evidence of foul play. Is there any way we can search the locker room?"

"Of course," the dean agreed. "Just let me check with Coach Mitchell."

He returned a few moments later, motioning for the girls to accompany him. Coach Mitchell caught up with them just as they were entering the men's locker room. "Let me find the locker-room attendant. He might know something," he said, slightly breathless from running.

A few minutes later the attendant came rushing in. Nancy could tell that he was flustered as he pointed out Randy's locker and, after checking a master list for the lock combination, opened it for the dean.

As Nancy watched carefully, Dean Jarvis sorted through the contents of Randy's locker: his clothes, towels, powder, a comb and brush, and a sports magazine. Nothing unusual.

Not that that was surprising. After all, Randy himself wasn't the one under suspicion, as far as Nancy was concerned.

"Wait a minute," she said as the attendant was turning to leave. "I know this may sound like a weird request, but could we check the lockers of *all* the players?" she asked Dean Jarvis.

Coach Mitchell's face turned bright red, and he sputtered, "If you're trying to say that any of my players would—"

"It's very unlikely, I know," Nancy put in

quickly. "But don't you think we ought to be absolutely certain?"

"She has a point," Dean Jarvis told the coach. Before Coach Mitchell could object again, the dean waved over the locker-room attendant and instructed him to open the other players' lockers.

Twenty lockers later, Nancy hadn't turned up anything more suspicious than a bunch of sports equipment and smelly towels. She heard Coach Mitchell mutter something under his breath about wasting time, but she held her tongue.

Nancy was disappointed. She knew there had to be some shred of evidence that would lead her to the person trying to hurt Randy, but it kept eluding her. For now, she had many questions— and no real answers.

"Not bad for cafeteria food!" Bess said as she popped a spoonful of spumoni into her mouth.

It was Italian night in the dining room. Bess had moved on to dessert, but Nancy and Ned were still finishing up their plates of baked lasagna.

"I wonder what happened to Jerry?" said Bess, turning her head to search the huge room.

Ned checked his watch. "He was supposed to meet us here half an hour ago." Ned checked his watch again, then scanned the crowded dining hall. "There he is now!" He stood up and waved Jerry over to the table. "You're late, buddy."

"I know." Jerry gave Bess an apologetic glance

as he pulled out a chair. "Sorry. I just came from the gym. A bunch of the guys on the team were waiting to hear about Randy."

From the dark expression on Jerry's handsome face, Nancy could tell that the news wasn't good. She herself had called the hospital right after the accident but had been told he was still being revived. "Is he okay?"

"He was released from the hospital, if that's what you mean," Jerry answered, still frowning.

"Thank goodness!" exclaimed Bess. "After seeing him fall flat, I didn't know what to think."

If the news was good, Nancy thought, then why was Jerry acting upset? "Will he be playing in Sunday's game?" she asked him.

"It looks that way, but the rest of the team is pretty shaken up." Jerry paused, pushing a lock of brown hair off his forehead. "The hospital's lab tests revealed that Randy's water bottle was laced with sleeping pills."

"Drugs!" Bess gasped. "That's horrible."

Nancy nodded. She'd suspected as much when she turned in Randy's water bottle.

"The doctors said he'll be able to play on Sunday," Jerry continued, "but the team's all torn apart. Some of the guys think Randy is crumbling under the stress and that he took the pills to quiet his nerves. Others are saying that he was poisoned." Jerry let out a low whistle. "Can you imagine that?"

Nancy could, but before she could respond, she

saw Coach Mitchell passing by with a tray of food in his hands.

"Coach," she called. When she caught his eye, he paused beside their table. "We just heard about Randy. You must be relieved that he's okay."

The coach shook his head. "I understand about stress, but there's no excuse for using drugs," he said with disgust. "The Wildcats will never make it with a quarterback who's cracking up."

Cracking up? Nancy frowned. It wasn't fair for the coach to assume that Randy had knowingly taken the drugs. Didn't the coach have any faith in him?

"As far as I'm concerned," Coach Mitchell added, "Randy Simpson's football career is in serious trouble."

Chapter

Nine

HOW CAN YOU be sure that Randy willingly took those sleeping pills?" Nancy asked the coach. "Has anyone spoken to him about it?"

"The doctors questioned him." Coach Mitchell frowned and rested his dinner tray on their table. "He denied it, of course. I suppose he's pretty embarrassed about passing out during practice."

"But if Randy wanted to take pills to ease his nerves, wouldn't he have taken the proper dosage?" Nancy asked, tuning out the noise of the busy room. "And why would he have dissolved the pills in his water bottle?"

"I don't know the answer to that, but if it were up to me, he'd be suspended from the team," the coach said. "But Dean Jarvis has decided that he deserves another chance." He lifted his tray and stepped back. "Now if you'll excuse me, I'm meeting my son for dinner."

As the coach disappeared into the crowd, Bess took another spoonful of her spumoni and said, "Coach Mitchell's being awfully hard on Randy."

Nancy nodded her agreement. "It's as if he doesn't want Randy to play on Sunday."

"Well, he is a college coach," Ned pointed out. "He can hardly condone a player using drugs."

"And to be fair," Jerry added, "Coach Mitchell is tough on all of us, even his son. The guy's a slavedriver, but that's his job—to whip us into shape."

Ned and Jerry had a point, Nancy realized. "Maybe the coach is just doing his job, but one thing about this case is becoming very clear. Someone really is trying to play 'kill the quarterback.'"

Confusion showed in Jerry's green eyes. "What do you mean, Nancy? I didn't know you were working on a case."

An awkward silence fell as Nancy stared first at Bess and then at Ned. "Nancy didn't want to say anything about it before—" Ned began to explain.

"I promised Randy that I'd keep things under wraps," Nancy added quickly. "But now that I'm officially working on the case, we could use your help. Someone has been threatening Randy. He's been told to throw Sunday's game—or else."

"You are kidding, right?" Jerry's mouth dropped open in astonishment as Nancy told him about the phone calls, the note, and the suspicious incidents. "Do the other football players know about this?" he asked.

"Not to my knowledge. That's why I need your help. I've been checking out possible suspects, but I haven't gotten an inside line on any of the Wildcats. Have you noticed anything strange going on among your teammates?"

Jerry hesitated for a moment, and Nancy could tell it troubled him to think of his teammates as possible suspects. "Not really," he answered at last. "I don't know anyone who openly has a gripe against him. Simpson's never going to make it to the pros, but he gives it his best shot. The guys admire him for that."

"I can't help thinking that I missed something in the locker room," Nancy murmured, twisting a strand of her reddish blond hair around a finger. "I was with the coach and Dean Jarvis when they searched the lockers, but there must be some sort of equipment closet or something."

"There sure is," said Jerry.

Nancy stood up abruptly. "Well, I'd better check on it. Anyone care to come along?"

"Count me out," Jerry said apologetically. "I have to get in some study time. But I'll see you all at our party."

"Party?" Bess sat up straighter in her chair. "Did I miss something?"

Grinning at Bess, Jerry said, "Not yet, but if you don't come I'll never forgive you. Our fraternity is throwing a bash tonight."

"Great," Bess told him, blushing. "We'll be there."

"In the meantime maybe I should go with you two to the locker room," Ned volunteered. "I don't want any of the guys on the team to freak out if they see you there."

Ten minutes later they were back in the sports complex. With Ned and Bess keeping watch at the locker room door, Nancy combed through the closet where the team equipment was stored. One by one, she examined the water bottles stacked on a tray. Although they were a little smudged and worn with use, nothing seemed amiss.

Next, Nancy sifted through the contents of the first-aid case. It was filled with ointments and bandages, but she noted that the only drug it contained was aspirin. Otherwise, the closet held only extra equipment, towels, stopwatches, and the like. No typewriter and no sleeping pills.

When she was finished, Nancy leaned against a row of lockers. "Hey, you guys," she called to Ned and Bess. "I need to talk through this case out loud." Sometimes simply bouncing ideas off other people helped her to unearth important clues.

Ned and Bess came into the locker room and sat on a bench opposite Nancy. "If all these events are related—and that's still an *if*," she began, "then someone had to be close enough to drop drugs in Randy's water bottle, pour kerosene on the wooden platform, and rig that barbell in the weight room."

"So the culprit is probably someone who can move about freely on campus," Bess surmised.

"Right," said Nancy. "Someone like Danielle Graves. Or Tamara Carlson. Both girls had access to the platform and to the weight room."

"But what about the drugs?" Bess pointed out. "Do you think any of those girls could talk her way into the guys' locker room?"

"That would be tough," Ned said.

"Maybe they didn't have to," Nancy suggested. "They were on the field this afternoon, at cheerleading practice. Susannah was there, too. If Tamara or Susannah is working with Zip, that gives them motive *and* opportunity.

"There are two team members we should keep in mind, too," Nancy added. "Josh and his father."

"Coach?" Ned's expression was extremely skeptical. "I don't know about that, Nan."

"He and Josh have a reason to want Randy off the roster," Nancy pointed out. She told Ned and

Bess about the conversation she'd overheard between Coach Mitchell and Dean Jarvis. "If Randy's out of the running, the coach has a shot at getting his son in as quarterback in Sunday's game."

"But he and Josh are one of the most sought-after athletic combos in college football," Ned protested.

Bess turned to Ned and asked, "Where were they before they came to Emerson?"

"Last year they were at Baldwin State," he answered. "Their team made it to the state finals. And Jerry says the Wildcats have a good chance of making it to the finals this year. At least, they did before Josh was put on probation."

Bess had been counting on her fingers as Nancy spoke. Now holding up her hand, she said, "Nan, that makes six suspects!"

"And we have very little time to figure out who is guilty," Nancy added soberly. "The homecoming game is the day after tomorrow."

Just then Josh Mitchell jogged in and grabbed a towel from his locker. Covered in sweat and breathing hard, he had obviously been working out. He said hello to Ned, then froze as his gaze lit on Nancy and Bess.

"Girls!" Josh made a point of looking around. "Hey, did I walk into the wrong locker room?" he teased.

"We were, uh, just on our way out," Nancy

said cautiously. She didn't want them to draw attention to her investigation.

"Nancy Drew and Bess, right?" Josh said, smiling. "Don't leave because of me. I'm going right back to the weight room. I just came in to grab a towel." Looking at Nancy, he added, "Dad told me about your investigation. He said—"

Josh was interrupted by a loud rumbling from the wall near the shower room. For a moment the entire room seemed to shake. Then, just as suddenly, the rumbling subsided.

"What was that?" Bess inquired.

"Believe it or not, that was the boiler kicking on," Josh explained, wiping his forehead with his towel. "My father has been trying to get that thing fixed for months. They say it's safe, but it sounds awful."

Bess giggled nervously. "I thought we were having an earthquake."

Josh slung the towel around his neck and faced Nancy. "As I was saying, Dad told me about Randy's close call in the weight room. We're all upset about him passing out this afternoon, too. I just wanted to let you know that I'll help you in any way I can. If you need a hand, just yell."

"Thanks for the offer," Nancy told him. "At the moment there's only one question I'd like you to answer. Did anyone ever threaten you before you went on academic probation?"

"Nope." Josh shook his head. "Never."

Hmm, thought Nancy. Apparently, the attacker was only interested in having Emerson lose the homecoming game. And whoever it was was willing to take drastic steps to make sure the Wildcats didn't win.

Nancy checked her watch. "Oops! We'd better get back to our room and change, Bess. It's already seven-thirty."

"And our party starts at eight," said Ned. "I'd better go, too."

"I had no idea." Bess grabbed Nancy's arm and pulled her toward the locker-room door. "See you later!"

"Let's sit out this song," Nancy said to Ned, leaning close to him. They had been dancing since Nancy and Bess arrived at the Omega Chi Epsilon fraternity an hour earlier. "I need to take a breather."

"Whatever you say, boss," Ned joked.

They threaded a path through the jumble of students dancing and milling around the living room. Bess, pretty in a maroon miniskirt and black sweater and boots, was sitting with Jerry on the steps leading to the second floor.

Adjusting the black-beaded belt of her cobalt blue silk jumpsuit, Nancy headed toward them. "Hi, guys," she said as Ned gave Jerry a high-five.

"I thought you were going to dance until you dropped," Bess said. "Isn't this party great?"

"How about some cider?" Ned suggested.

Nancy and Bess both nodded, and Jerry went with Ned to get it.

"I've been wanting to talk with you," a voice said behind Nancy.

Turning, Nancy found herself face-to-face with Danielle Graves.

"It's—it's about Randy," Danielle added.

"Oh? What about him?" Nancy inquired, keeping her voice level.

Danielle's face seemed unnaturally pale in the living room's artificial light. "I was there when he—when he collapsed this afternoon, and I heard that you were trying to find out who's after him. . . ." Her voice trailed off, and she swallowed hard.

"Listen, Nancy, I know I said positively wicked things about Randy," Danielle continued. "And he deserved them—"

"Because he broke up with you?" Bess put in.

"Well, yes," she admitted. "I was mad, and I wanted to get back at him. But not *that* way. I wanted to make him feel bad for breaking up with me, but I'd never really try to hurt a guy with fire or drugs or anything. You know?"

"I think I understand what you're saying," Nancy said slowly.

Danielle seemed genuinely upset about Randy and obviously regretted her outbursts, Nancy thought as the petite girl wandered off. But Nancy had no proof that this wasn't just an act.

She forgot all about the case a moment later, however, as Ned reappeared beside her. She took the mug of hot cider he held out, and the two of them found a spot on the stairs behind Bess and Jerry.

"Nice party, Nickerson," she murmured, leaning in close to him.

"And you're the nicest thing about it." Ned's arm circled tightly around her, and his lips closed on hers in a kiss that took Nancy's breath away.

The rest of the party passed pleasantly with dancing and talking. Nancy was surprised when it was midnight and time to return to their dorm. By the time they said their final good-nights to Ned and Jerry in the lobby of the dorm, however, Nancy realized how tired she was.

"I'm beat," she said as they walked down the hall to their suite. "Oh, hi, Tamara," she said as the pretty, dark-skinned girl came up behind them in the hallway, wearing a nightgown and bathrobe.

"Hi, Bess, Nancy." Tamara smiled at them before disappearing into her room.

Taking her room key from her purse, Nancy unlocked the door and pushed it open, then reached inside to flick on the light. As she stepped into the room, the first thing she noticed was a piece of lined yellow paper on the carpet.

"Someone must have slipped this under the door," she said, reaching down to pick it up. Nancy unfolded the note and read it.

SCHOOL'S OUT FOR YOU, NANCY DREW. LEAVE EMERSON——BEFORE IT'S TOO LATE!

Chapter

Ten

Nᴀɴᴄʏ ꜰᴇʟᴛ the blood drain from her face. Quickly rereading the note, she handed it to Bess. "Someone doesn't want me on this case," she said, frowning.

"It's a threat," Bess said worriedly. "I don't like this, Nancy."

"Well, it's not going to work." With a determined jab, Nancy reached into her bag for the note Randy had received. She sat down on the sofa and spread out the two notes on the table, then peered from one to the other. Although one was on white paper and the other on yellow, they were both typed using only capital letters.

Suddenly she leaned forward. "Hey, look at this. The capital *E* in each note is the same. The bottom of it is broken off." She pointed to the *E*'s in both her note and Randy's. "These were definitely typed on the same typewriter."

"Which means that you're really in danger," Bess said with a quaver. "Oh, Nan, maybe we should leave in the morning. We don't have to stay all weekend."

"We can't leave just because things are heating up," Nancy protested. She leaned forward to study the notes once again. "If I could just find the machine that these were typed on . . ."

Bess rolled her eyes. "Oh, sure, it'll only take a few hundred years to try out every typewriter on campus," she teased.

Shooting her friend a challenging glance, Nancy said, "We don't have to try every typewriter," she said. "But some of our suspects do happen to live right in this dorm. We can't check Tamara's room, since we know she's in there now. But she's not our only suspect."

"You mean Danielle? But what if she's in her room?" Bess asked nervously.

Nancy grabbed Bess and pulled her toward the door. "There's only one way to find out."

A few minutes later, after checking the directory in the lobby, the girls were walking stealthily down the empty third-floor hallway.

"Here it is," Bess whispered. "Three fourteen."

Holding her breath, Nancy knocked on the door. There was no answer. "Perfect," she said, kneeling and pulling her lockpick set from her purse. A moment later she had the lock clicking open.

"Okay, you wait in the lounge by the elevator," she instructed. "And—"

"And if Danielle comes, I'll stall her," Bess finished. "We've already been over this, Nan. Don't worry about me. Just hurry!"

As Bess went back down the hall, Nancy slipped into Danielle's room and turned on the light. She glanced quickly around the small room, taking in the dresser, bed, desk, and closet.

Going methodically around the room, she searched them all, checking for a typewriter or for anything that could hold kerosene. She even opened the makeup jars on top of Danielle's dresser, but she didn't find anything unusual.

After ten minutes Nancy made herself stop and take a deep breath. There should at least be a typewriter, she thought. Where was it?

She froze as she heard footsteps in the hall outside, but a moment later they passed by. That was when Nancy's gaze lit on the small computer on Danielle's desk. Of course, she thought. Danielle wrote her papers on her computer.

She leaned against Danielle's desk, thinking. There was no way she had time to turn the thing on and figure out how to print something. From what she knew of computer printouts, though, it would be unusual for any computer to type an imperfection such as the broken *E* in the threatening notes.

It was too soon to take Danielle off her list of suspects, Nancy knew, but the cheerleader was now taking a backseat to Zip, Susannah, and Tamara.

Nancy gasped as she checked her watch. She'd been in the room more than fifteen minutes! Putting her ear to the door, Nancy waited until she was sure there was no one around, then she slipped back into the empty hallway.

The next morning Bess was trying to get Nancy to move faster. Bess grabbed her denim jacket off the back of her chair in the student center, where she and Nancy had just finished a quick, late breakfast of muffins and hot cocoa. "Come on, Nan. I don't want to miss the fair. It's ten-thirty already."

"Just a minute," Nancy told her. "I have to call Dean Jarvis. There's something I'd like to find out about Susannah Carlson."

The girls found a campus phone in the student center's entrance. Checking the campus directory that hung from the booth by a cord, Nancy called Dean Jarvis's extension. It was Saturday, but to Nancy's relief, the dean was in.

"This is a delicate matter," Dean Jarvis said after she told him what she wanted to know. "But if it'll help your case, I guess I can tell you. Let me access the file." He put her on hold, and Nancy drummed her fingers against the phone until he came back on the line. "Ms. Carlson was dismissed from Emerson because of a failing grade-point average," the dean told her.

"She flunked out?" Nancy took a moment to digest the information. "Is there anything else unusual in her record?"

She heard the dean put the phone back down as he keyed in something more. "That's all the information I have."

Nancy thanked him, then hung up. "So that's why Susannah holds such a grudge against Emerson," she said to Bess after relating what she'd just found out. "But this doesn't in any way indicate that she would go after Randy to get back at Emerson. I can't believe she'd do it, but I am going to have to search Tamara's room today anyway."

"After the fair," Bess insisted, grabbing Nancy's arm. "Like it or not, Drew, you're going to have some fun today!"

From the student center the girls headed straight for the oval. They overtook Tamara and Zip, who were walking on the path just ahead of them. In their dark jeans, high-top sneakers, and short leather jackets, they looked great, Nancy thought.

"Zip looks different without his Russell letter jacket," she whispered to Bess.

As they rounded the corner of Ivy Hall, Nancy glimpsed a colorful array of tables and booths. Everything from sweaters to pottery to pillows to leather bags and belts were on sale, and thick crowds of students jammed each booth.

"Nancy!"

Hearing Ned's familiar voice, Nancy spun around to see her handsome boyfriend, wearing faded blue jeans and an Emerson basketball jacket, jog toward her.

Swinging Nancy around in a hug, he said, "Sorry I missed you at breakfast. I had to go over the order of the floats for the parade this afternoon."

"That's okay." While Bess wandered among the booths, Nancy told Ned about the note she'd received.

"Bess is right—you are in danger," Ned said gravely when she was done. "Promise you'll be careful, okay?"

"I always am," Nancy said, giving him a hug. "What's the latest on Randy?" she asked, eager to change the subject.

"He says he's feeling fine. He's even going to ride on the team float—"

"This fair is great," said Bess, moving back to them. She held up a sweater with colorful geometric designs on it in one hand, and a belt in the other. "Look what I bought."

"Uh-oh. Everyone better move fast, before you buy out the whole fair," Nancy teased.

Bess grinned. "You know I can't resist a bargain."

Bess broke off as she heard a cry.

"Help! Help me!"

Spinning around, Nancy glimpsed a flurry of motion behind the shiny glass facade of the modern library building that stood on the opposite side of the oval. Someone had opened one of the windows on the third story. In the open space, she could see two figures struggling.

Nancy squinted, trying to follow the action. Her breath caught in her throat as one of the figures was pushed out the library window an instant later. Beside her, Bess let out a bloodcurdling scream.

A young man wearing an Emerson football team jacket was now dangling from the window ledge! His attacker shoved him, apparently trying to push him from the building.

There was nothing for the player to cling to on the building's sleek facade except the window ledge.

And there was nothing but cold, hard pavement three stories below the window.

Chapter

Eleven

Hey—someone's trying to kill Randy!" Bess shouted.

Her heart pounding, Nancy took off at a flat-out run for the library. She was halfway to it when she glanced up again and noticed that the player had shiny blond hair.

It wasn't Randy but Josh Mitchell dangling there. The figure struggling with Josh was dressed in dark colors, and it looked as if his head was covered with a black ski mask.

As Nancy raced on, the figure inside continued to try to dislodge Josh. Then, suddenly, the attacker disappeared from view. Josh dangled for only a moment longer, then pulled himself inside. An audible sigh of relief rippled through the crowd on the oval.

By the time Nancy reached the door of the library, Ned was beside her. Together they raced inside and stopped short in front of the two elevators, checking the indicator lights above the doors. One car was ascending. The other seemed to be stopped in the basement.

"The stairs!" Nancy cried, nodding across the modern lobby to a sleek wood-and-metal staircase on the far side. "You stay here and stop anyone wearing dark clothes."

Nancy raced to the stairs, her muscles screaming as she climbed two flights. She didn't pass anyone on the stairway. As Nancy hurried past the desks, book stacks, and study modules on the third floor, she finally spotted Josh. He was leaning against a table near the window, breathing hard. A handful of students and librarians were clustered around him.

"Josh, are you okay?" Nancy asked.

He glanced at her, obviously disoriented. "Yeah. Just kind of shook up." Josh swallowed as he straightened the collar of his shirt. "Did you see that creep?" he asked the crowd, scanning the nearby aisles of books. "Where did he go?"

"I didn't see anybody," said a blond-haired girl, "but I was doing research on the other side of the floor."

"Did *any* of you see Josh's attacker?" Nancy asked each of them. They all shook their heads.

Nancy didn't wait to hear any more. Josh's attacker was getting away! She walked carefully down the wide center aisle, checking each narrower aisle of bookcases. She saw no one and decided that the attacker had already left the floor. Racing down to the second floor, then the first, Nancy searched each carefully. There were only a few students, and none of them was wearing dark clothing.

"Any luck, Ned?" Nancy asked as she rejoined her boyfriend by the first-floor elevator bank.

He shook his head. "No one came out. I guess with all the homecoming festivities, today isn't a big study day on campus. A bunch of people from the fair took the elevator up to see what had happened, though. They included Dean Jarvis and a couple of security guards."

Nancy let out a sigh of frustration. "It looks like our guy got away. All he had to do was take that ski mask off to fit in. We'll never be able to pick him out now." Running a hand through her hair, she added, "Come on, let's go back up to Josh."

"I'm afraid I can't," Ned said apologetically. "I hate to desert you, but I have to get over to the floats."

"That's okay," Nancy told him. "Bess and I will meet you at the student center for lunch at noon."

When Nancy returned to the third floor, Josh was surrounded by a larger crowd, which included his father, Dean Jarvis, and two campus security guards. Nancy also noticed Bess standing on the fringe of the group, talking with Zip and Tamara.

Josh seemed to be recounting the details of the attack. "I was sitting at this table, working on a paper, when a guy came up and grabbed me by the collar."

"Did he say anything?" Coach Mitchell asked his son, shoving his hands in the pockets of his navy warmup suit.

Josh nodded. "He told me that Emerson had to lose Sunday's game. After that he dragged me to the window and—you know the rest."

That was the same threat Randy had received, Nancy thought. Didn't the culprit realize that Josh was suspended from the team roster?

"This business is getting out of hand," Dean Jarvis stated. "If I had my druthers, I'd cancel that game."

"Not the homecoming game!" someone said.

"Dean Jarvis," the coach began, "we have hundreds of alumni visiting campus this week. I don't think it would be wise to disappoint them by calling off the game."

"We can't buckle under now," Josh added. "I know that this guy is trying to scare the team. But we can't give him that satisfaction."

Just then two police officers strode up. Dean Jarvis quickly explained what had happened to Josh and filled the officers in on the earlier attacks against Randy. "I'm considering calling the president to cancel the game, officers. Any advice?"

One of the officers, a gray-haired man with a bristly mustache, shrugged, saying, "There's no guarantee that this kook will stop being a menace, even if you do cancel the game."

The second officer—the name on his badge was Pulaski, Nancy noted—was writing vigorously on a clipboard. "Did you recognize this person's voice?" Officer Pulaski asked Josh.

"No. I'm sure it was a man, but the voice wasn't familiar."

That made sense, Nancy thought to herself. She hadn't gotten a clear look at the menacing figure, but it would require a lot of strength to physically try to toss Josh out the window. That would probably rule out Danielle and Susannah.

Officer Pulaski tapped his pen against his clipboard. "Out of ink." He looked over at Josh. "Do you have a pen, kid?"

Josh checked his pockets, then shrugged. "Nothing to write with. Sorry."

Coach Mitchell reached into his jacket and handed the officer a pen. "Now," said Officer Pulaski. "Can you describe what the assailant was wearing?"

"His face was covered with a black ski mask . . ." Josh began. His voice trailed off, and Nancy noticed that his eyes were focused on something in the crowd.

A moment later he pointed at Zip Williams. He said, "There. He was dressed just like that— in dark clothes."

Nancy glanced critically at Zip. His clothes were right, and he certainly had the motive, but he also had an alibi. She had seen him down at the fair just before the attack.

The crowd was silent as the two quarterbacks glared at each other. Zip sneered, then turned and stalked off indignantly, with Tamara right behind him.

Tension hung in the air for a long, silent moment. Finally Dean Jarvis addressed the crowd. "Josh is okay, and the homecoming game will go on as scheduled," he announced. "Now let's all move off and leave this matter to the police."

As the crowd began to disperse, Nancy and Bess lingered behind to hear the police finish their questioning of Josh.

"Ready to go, son?" Coach Mitchell asked as Officer Pulaski tucked his clipboard under his arm. "Let's get out of here and grab something to eat."

As the officers and the Mitchells headed for the elevators, Nancy found herself staring at the empty table. Something about it disturbed her, but she couldn't pinpoint what it was. She glanced over at Josh, then back at the table. Finally it hit her.

"That's strange," she said aloud. When Bess

met her eyes, she explained. "Josh said he was sitting here studying, but he didn't have any papers or books with him. In fact, he didn't even have a pen to lend that police officer."

"No wonder he's such a lousy student," Bess commented.

Nancy thoughtfully drummed her fingers on the table. Could it be that simple? Or had Josh lied about coming there to study?

Come on, Drew! she chastised herself the next second. Josh was practically thrown from a library window. Give the guy a break!

Shaking herself from her thoughts, Nancy turned to Bess. "We might as well go back down to the fair."

The girls made their way downstairs and back to the crowded oval. They threaded their way past the booths, but Nancy hardly paid any attention to the items for sale. Her mind was focused on the details of the case.

Someone was after Randy—and now it looked as if that person was after Josh, too. The message had been consistent—lose Sunday's game.

What was so important about that game? Someone was going to an awful lot of trouble to make sure that Emerson lost. Maybe it was Susannah's way of getting revenge against Emerson or Zip's incredible need to win.

But each of their motives seemed flimsy in light of the seriousness of the crimes. Whoever was behind the attacks was willing to murder in order to make sure Emerson lost the big game. Nancy couldn't help thinking there was some important piece missing from the puzzle.

"Nan!" Bess's urgent whisper tore Nancy from her thoughts. "The police are back!"

"What?" Following Bess's gaze, Nancy spotted Officer Pulaski and his gray-haired partner walking across the oval with a purposeful stride. They wove around a family with two young toddlers, then cut across the lawn.

A moment later the police stepped up to Zip Williams, who was leaning against a tree at the edge of the oval, talking with Tamara.

"Come on," said Nancy, grabbing Bess's arm and pulling her toward the group.

As soon as Zip saw the police, he stood up straight and dropped his girlfriend's hand. Nancy saw him stiffen as Officer Pulaski clapped a hand on his shoulder and spoke to him.

"You're wanted for questioning down at the station."

Chapter

Twelve

WHAT'S GOING ON?" Tamara demanded to know, placing a hand protectively on Zip's arm.

"I didn't do anything." Zip shook himself free of Officer Pulaski's grip.

"We're not arresting you," the gray-haired man told Zip. "We just want to ask you a few questions."

Nancy could see the fury in Zip's black eyes, but he managed to restrain himself. "I'll cooperate," he said firmly, "but I'm telling you, I know nothing about Josh."

Tamara watched tearfully as her boyfriend left with the officers. Then she turned and ran from the oval.

"How awful!" Bess said. "I don't know about

you, but that just made me lose my enthusiasm for the fair."

"Me, too," Nancy agreed. "I can't believe they'll hold him, though. Anyway, we have to go meet Ned and Jerry for lunch."

Soon they were sitting with the guys in the student center, their plates piled high with Mexican food.

"I feel sorry for Zip," Bess was saying as she spooned chili into her mouth, "but I don't know what to believe—especially since he disappeared right before the masked man struck."

"What did you say?" Nancy asked suddenly, pausing with a nacho in midair.

"Zip disappeared from the oval," Bess repeated. "You remember how we saw him walking with Tamara on the way over to the fair? Well, a little while later I saw him jog off along the path beside Ivy Hall. He still hadn't returned when you ran off to help Josh."

"So Zip *doesn't* have an alibi," Nancy said excitedly, thinking aloud. "This changes everything. Zip could be the masked man."

"He must be the one behind all these threats!" Jerry said excitedly.

Nancy nodded. "If he worked with Susannah or Tamara, they could get access to the Wildcats' equipment—and to the weight room."

Jerry put down his soda and snapped his fingers. "It's *got* to be him."

"Whoa, buddy!" Ned said, putting up a hand. "Let's not jump to conclusions. Does he match the description that Josh gave to the police?"

"Perfectly," Nancy told him, "except for the ski mask, but he could have easily ditched that. Isn't it funny that Zip didn't wear his red-and-white Russell team jacket today? It would have stood out more than dark clothing. But if he was planning a crime, his team jacket would have been a dead giveaway."

Ned bit into a chip with salsa on it, then said, "There's only one problem. Why would Zip attack Josh when he's not even going to be playing in the game?"

"I wondered the same thing," said Nancy. "Maybe the attacker was using Josh to send a message to the whole team. You know, what happened to him could happen to any of them. In any case, I think Jerry's on the right track," she continued. "With Zip at the police station, half the case might be solved."

"What about the other half?" asked Bess.

"That's our job," Nancy said with a smile. At last it seemed that the investigation was coming together. "It's time to pay Tamara Carlson's room a little visit."

After lunch the guys headed out to take care of final preparations for the float parade. The wind had died down, and Nancy felt warm as she and Bess went back to Packard Hall.

As they passed through the lobby of the dorm, Nancy spotted Danielle Graves sitting on a sofa in the lounge. She was nose to nose with a football player, who seemed smitten with her fluttering lashes and lilting laughter.

"Did you see that?" Bess whispered as soon as they were in the elevator.

"Looks like Danielle has gotten over Randy," Nancy said with a smile. "I'm beginning to rule her out as a suspect. There's no way she could have made that attack on Josh in the library. Besides, we didn't find anything in her room."

When they reached the fifth floor, Nancy went straight to Tamara's door. The door opened on her second knock, and Susannah poked her head out.

"Hi, Nancy. Hi, Bess," Susannah said. There was a worried look on her face as she ushered the girls into Tamara's room. Emerson banners and museum posters hung on the walls, and colorful pillows were scattered on the bed. A desk stood against the wall next to the window. "Have you heard?"

Nancy nodded as she and Bess sat on the bed. "We were there when the police came. That's why we stopped by," she said, mentally crossing her fingers. "To see how Tamara's taking it."

"Not so great," Susannah told them. "She went down to the police station to wait for Zip. I just hate to see this happen to him."

As Susannah spoke, Nancy glanced down at the desk. It took her a moment to realize that what she wanted to check was sitting right there. The typewriter!

"And Tam is so unhappy!" Susannah exclaimed. She shook her head sadly, staring down at the floor.

Nancy took advantage of the opportunity to nudge Bess and nod at the typewriter on the desk. *Type a letter!* she mouthed.

"If there's anything we can do, just let us know," Nancy told Susannah.

"Well, we should let you get back to work," Bess added, getting to her feet. She walked over to the desk and ran a finger along the shiny edge of the typewriter. "Looks like you've been doing a lot of typing."

"Oh, just some correspondence." Susannah waved at the papers dismissively. "My handwriting is awful, so I type everything. Tam's been letting me use her typewriter."

"Do you think I could use it for a quick note?" Bess flashed Susannah a winning smile. "I have rotten handwriting, too, and I've been wanting to write this letter—to my boyfriend, Jerry. It's sort of a love letter."

Way to go, Bess! Nancy cheered silently.

Bess picked up a blank piece of paper and slipped it into the typewriter. "I'll make it short," she said sweetly.

An amused grin lit Susannah's face. "Be my guest."

Pushing down the button to lock in the capital letters, Bess pursed her lips and began typing. Nancy forced herself not to watch while Bess pecked out one line, then two, then three. . . .

"I thought you'd never finish that letter!" Nancy whispered when they had stepped back into their suite and closed the door.

"I got carried away," Bess said with a sheepish grin.

Nancy sat down on the couch and glanced down at the two threatening notes that still lay on the coffee table. Then, holding out her hand to Bess, she said expectantly, "Well?"

"Read it and weep!" Bess giggled as she handed Nancy the note.

The first words were "DEAREST JERRY." Nancy's heart pounded in anticipation as she compared the *E*'s to those in the threatening notes.

"They don't match," she announced, fighting back disappointment. "The typeface on Tamara's machine is more angular, and the *E* is solid." She frowned as she looked up at Bess. "Chances are, these hate letters did not come from Susannah or Tamara. Unless they have access to another typewriter, and that's pretty unlikely."

"So what does it mean?" Bess asked.

Shrugging, Nancy said, "I doubt Zip could have managed all those attacks on his own, which means my biggest suspects are probably innocent. I've got to do some more digging!"

"That's all very interesting," Bess said impatiently. "But what about my note? You didn't even read it!"

Nancy took a closer look:

DEAREST JERRY,
MY LITTLE SNICKERDOODLE!
WILL YOU EVER KNOW HOW I LOOOOOVE YOU SOOOO?
WHENEVER I SLEEP, I DREAM OF YOU . . .

"You're too much, Bess!" Nancy laughed, unable to read any more of it.

"Aren't I?" Bess said proudly. "Personally, I think it's a masterpiece." She reached for the note, but Nancy tugged it away.

Her blue eyes sparkled as she said, "Really? And how would you feel if I passed this masterpiece along to dearest Jerry?"

"Nancy, you wouldn't!" The color drained from Bess's face.

"No, I guess not," Nancy relented, handing the note back to Bess. "We'd better get going," she added. "Ned will kill us if we're late for the parade."

* * *

"Wow!" Bess exclaimed a half-hour later. "The floats look so huge! Like giant toys."

She and Nancy were sitting on a low brick wall along the homecoming parade route. The street was lined with students, people from nearby towns, and alumni of all ages.

Nancy stared up at the float that was passing in front of them, a fifteen-foot-high globe of the world that actually turned on its axis. "They are pretty amazing."

"Here comes the drill team float. Look at the roses!" Bess jumped up and pointed at the giant cake. "My design looks fabulous, doesn't it?"

"Definitely," Nancy agreed. She waved at Kristin Seidel as the blond girl marched by in her purple-and-orange majorette's uniform.

"Hi!" Bess joined in, waving an Emerson pennant that she had bought.

The drill team's giant cake disappeared around a corner and was followed by a bagpipe band. Then came the float bearing the homecoming king and queen.

"Those thrones are great," Bess commented, pointing to decorated golden chairs on the float. Behind the thrones were trellises threaded with real roses.

"And Jerry was right. The king does have to wear purple tights!" Nancy added with a laugh.

The next float was built by the football team and displayed a huge replica of a football. Nancy shook her head as the papier-mâché-and-wood model rolled down the street.

Anchored to a raised platform behind the giant football was a goalpost. Sitting on the goalpost's crossbar was Randy Simpson, his legs swinging freely in the air.

This was the first time Nancy had seen Randy since his accident. He seemed to be fine and was grinning easily as he waved at the cheering by-standers. The rest of the team hailed the crowd from the edges of the float.

"I think he sees us!" Bess jumped up and waved her pennant as Randy tossed them a salute.

Randy's expression changed a moment later, though, when the goalpost began to wobble as the float came to a corner. The color drained from his face as the raised platform began to rock back and forth.

"Oh, no!" Bess shrieked.

Nancy gasped. "It's going to fall right off the float!"

When the tractor and flatbed rounded the corner, the giant football tilted to one side and the raised platform lurched to the edge of the float. Randy lost his balance and slid off the crossbar but managed to grab it with his hands. He held on to the wildly swinging goalpost, but he couldn't stop its downward plunge.

Before any of the other players knew what was happening, the goalpost toppled off and crashed onto the street with a sickening crunch, taking Randy with it!

Chapter

Thirteen

Her heart in her throat, Nancy jumped down from the wall she and Bess had been sitting on.

"Poor Randy!" Bess cried, but Nancy was already halfway around the corner. She was only dimly aware of the shrieks from the crowd, her attention focused solely on getting to Randy. Pushing past the crowd that had gathered around the disabled float, Nancy rushed over to the mangled goalpost on the street. The giant football had fallen on top of it.

"Randy!" she called.

"Where is he?" Bess cried, right behind her.

At last Nancy heard Randy's muffled voice. "I'm under here!"

The football players joined Nancy and Bess, and they all tugged at the football and the goalpost. Randy was curled in a ball underneath them, his arms wrapped protectively around his head.

"I'm okay," he gasped, crawling out onto the street. He stood up and wiped his hands on his jeans, while his teammates pressed forward with concerned expressions.

"That was some fall!" Bess exclaimed.

Randy nodded, breathing deeply. "That's for sure. Luckily, one of the first things a quarterback learns is how to take a tumble."

Glancing up, Nancy saw that the parade was continuing despite the accident, moving around the Wildcats' ruined float. The tractor driver had pulled his vehicle off to the side, and now he came rushing over to them.

"I don't know how that happened," the short, rotund man said, obviously flustered. "Are you okay?" he asked Randy. "I nearly died when I heard that thing land. I don't get it. We weren't going that fast when we took that corner."

Nancy had been so worried about Randy that she hadn't even thought about that. Now that she did, something seemed very wrong about the whole accident. "The float started rocking *before* the turn," she pointed out.

Randy nodded. "It never did seem stable, but I just figured we were hitting lots of bumps."

Nancy tuned out the noise from a group of clowns that was parading by. Walking along the perimeter of the cracked football, she checked the holes that were drilled along its edge. "These were used to attach the football to the platform, right?"

The tractor driver nodded. "There are six studs on the platform. The studs go through those holes, and a bolt is secured on top to keep it in place."

"That's strange." Nancy sifted through the wreckage of the float until she found a metal bolt. "Is this one of the bolts?" she asked, holding it up.

"Yeah," the driver replied, scratching his head. "But there should be five others."

Nancy stared at the bolt. "I wonder what happened to them?"

While colorful floats curved around them, Nancy, Bess, and Randy carefully sifted through the wreckage of the float. They checked the road and the flatbed, but they didn't find any of the other bolts.

"Someone must have removed them," Nancy told Randy, frowning.

"That's what I figured," Randy mumbled, tugging angrily on the end of his football jersey. "But you know what? I'm not afraid anymore. I've had it with this creep! He made me look so bad with those pills." His dark eyes were sincere

111

as he added, "I don't take drugs, Nancy! Honest. I'm not about to screw up my life that way."

"I believe you, Randy," Nancy assured him. "But you're still in danger—now more than ever. The person who wants Emerson to lose tomorrow is obviously not going to stop these attacks. And the game is less than twenty-four hours away! With time running out, I'm afraid our culprit might resort to even more desperate measures."

She put a hand on Randy's shoulder, saying, "It's time to get more help from the college administration." Checking that no one could overhear, Nancy lowered her voice and told Randy about her investigation.

She finished up, "I need to do a thorough check of all the players on Emerson's team. If Dean Jarvis can help me cut through some red tape, I might have a chance to get this thing solved before tomorrow's game."

"I hope it's not one of the guys on the team," Randy said, "but you're the detective." With a weary smile, Randy made a fist. "Go for it, Nancy!"

Nancy turned to see Ned running up the street. Josh was jogging beside him.

"I came as soon as I heard what happened," he said breathlessly. "It's a good thing that you didn't get hurt, buddy," he said, clapping Randy on the back. "What happened?"

Nancy, Randy, and Bess all launched into an explanation at once. When Nancy told Ned about the missing bolts, his eyes glimmered with anger. "We've got to catch the guy who did this."

"I'll second that," Randy put in.

Nancy nodded. "Ned, can you check with other people who worked on floats in the shed, and ask if they saw anything suspicious? Maybe someone got a look at the person who tampered with the Wildcats' float."

Ned nodded. "I'll check it out right away. Everyone has to meet back at the shed to dismantle the floats." He nodded at Jerry and Josh. "We'll be tied up there for the rest of the afternoon, but I'll pick you up at seven for the dance."

"In the meantime," Nancy said, "I'm going to see if Dean Jarvis can help us."

"And I'm going to take a long, hot shower to recuperate from this parade," Randy added.

While Bess went back to the room to rest up for the dance, Nancy went to the office of the dean of students. Although he wasn't in, his secretary directed Nancy to the student center, where the dean was supervising the setup for that night's dance.

When Nancy arrived, she saw that lilac-colored tablecloths covered the cafeteria's round tables and that a vase of fresh asters had been placed in the center of each one. The room was empty except for the staff of caterers who were scurrying about. Dean Jarvis was standing next to the serving counter, talking to someone wearing a chef's cap. Nancy waited until they finished their conversation before approaching the dean.

"The decorations are beautiful," Nancy told him.

"Hello, Nancy," he said. "We try to put out a nice spread for our alumni." Folding his arms over his chest, he added, "But I'm guessing that it's not the dance preparations that bring you here."

"Good guess." Nancy told him about the float that had crashed into the street. "I was wondering if you could look up the records of some of the suspects and fill me in on anything unusual."

"That information's confidential—" Dean Jarvis began hesitantly.

"I understand that," Nancy cut in quickly. "I'm not asking to read anything. But it wouldn't break any rules for you to check, would it?" Noting the dean's frown, she tried another tack. "If you feel uncomfortable about releasing confidential information, you don't have to tell me. But, please, check the files. And if you find anything unusual, at least report it to the police."

Dean Jarvis stared down at the floor for a moment. Finally he looked up again and said, "You've got a deal." Pulling a small notepad from the breast pocket of his tweed jacket, he asked, "Now, who are the suspects?"

Nancy asked him to check on Tamara Carlson and recheck her sister Susannah's file. The dean jotted down their names. She also added all the members of the football team.

"I was also wondering about Emerson's first-string quarterback, Josh Mitchell," Nancy went on. "Maybe he thinks you'll let him play if Randy is injured."

"But Josh was nearly injured, too," the dean pointed out.

Nancy had been having second thoughts about Josh's accident, and now she spelled them out for the dean. "It looks that way," she said, "but I have my doubts. Josh definitely wasn't doing any studying in the library when he was attacked today. He didn't even have a pen with him, much less any books. It's possible that he worked with an accomplice and engineered the 'accident' to divert suspicion away from him."

She took a deep breath as she added, "I'm also wondering about Josh's father, Coach Mitchell. His motive could be the same as Josh's."

Dean Jarvis stopped writing and lowered his pad. "You suspect a member of our own faculty?"

His question made Nancy feel a little uncomfortable. "I know he doesn't have an obvious motive, but I'd rather double-check and be safe."

Frowning, Dean Jarvis wrote down the name. With a sigh, the dean closed his notepad and tucked it away. "All right, Nancy. I'll check the files on everyone—including the coach—if there's any chance of finding our menace."

Nancy grinned at him. "Thanks, Dean Jarvis."

"I have a special message for you," Bess said with a smile as soon as Nancy opened the door to their suite. Bess was sitting on the couch in the living room with a book in her lap and her feet tucked beneath her. She was in her pink terrycloth bathrobe, and a towel was wrapped turban-style around her hair.

"From a special guy?" Nancy inquired, raising her eyebrows.

"It's from your one and only," Bess confirmed, wiggling her eyebrows suggestively. "Ned has a surprise for you. Instead of picking you up, he wants to meet you at the entrance of College Woods in an hour."

"A surprise?" Nancy felt a delicious tingle. "I wonder what Nickerson is up to?"

"It sounds incredibly romantic to me," Bess gushed.

Nancy flew into her little bedroom and began peeling off her leather jacket, jeans, and turtleneck. "In that case, I guess I'd better start getting dressed!"

After a quick shower, Nancy pulled back her reddish blond hair in a French braid. She slipped on a green silk dress and matching belt, then applied just a touch of eye shadow and blush.

"How do I look, Bess?" she asked, going to the open doorway to the bathroom.

Still in her bathrobe, Bess was rubbing moisturizer on her face. Looking at Nancy's reflection in the mirror over the sink, she smiled and said, "Terrific! I love that color. It really brings out the blue in your eyes."

"Thanks." Nancy pulled a black blazer on over her dress. "Are you wearing the pink or the purple?" she asked, nodding to two dresses that hung on the inside of the bathroom door.

"I haven't decided," Bess moaned. "What do you think?"

"I think you'd better make a decision, or else you'll still be wearing your bathrobe when Jerry arrives," Nancy teased. "I'd better get going before Ned starts wondering what happened to me. See you at the dance!"

The air was cold when Nancy stepped out of the dorm. The sun had almost set, and a breeze rustled through the leaves, causing some of them to flutter down from the branches. Slipping her hands into the pockets of her blazer, Nancy headed toward the woods that swept down the hill to the lake.

As she walked along the path, Nancy passed a handful of students. Other than that, the path was fairly deserted. Most people must be on their way to the dance on the other side of the campus, Nancy realized.

A stout brick wall marked the entrance of

College Woods, and Nancy stopped by the gate. Now that she wasn't moving, she shivered from the cold. It was seven o'clock exactly, she saw, checking her watch. Ned should be there any second.

After five minutes of waiting, Nancy began to get impatient. She was hopping from foot to foot, trying to stay warm, when she noticed a figure approaching. At last!

On second glance, she realized that it wasn't Ned. It was Carrie, the girl who played the Emerson wildcat. She was dressed in her mascot costume.

"Hi, Carrie," Nancy called as the wildcat approached.

But the girl didn't respond. She rushed toward Nancy, lifting her hand high above her.

Something glinted in the pale moonlight. Nancy gasped as she realized what the object was. It was a knife—a shiny and sharp knife. And it was arcing through the air right toward her throat!

Chapter

Fourteen

HEY!" NANCY STAGGERED backward as the mascot swung the deadly blade at her.

Twisting to one side, she lifted her foot and aimed a kick at the mascot's arm. Her shoe struck the elbow, throwing the mascot back. As she stumbled, Nancy saw that the mascot's feet were large—too large to belong to a girl. And this person was wearing purple high-top sneakers. Whoever this was, it definitely *wasn't* Carrie!

To Nancy's dismay, her assailant had managed to keep hold of the knife. Spinning, Nancy took off up the path, back toward the dorm. She ran as fast as she could, but her black pumps kept slipping on the slick asphalt. Stealing a glance back, Nancy realized she couldn't outrun this creep—not in heels. He was only a few yards behind her!

Spotting a huge trash container, she veered off the path. Slow him down! The thought screamed through her mind. She grabbed the edge of the steel barrel and pushed. A second later it was rolling down the path.

The "wildcat" didn't see the barrel until it was too late. It struck him with a loud clatter, knocking him down to the pavement.

Without a moment to waste, Nancy raced ahead, grateful to have any sort of lead. Her heart was pounding, but she kept running. Her lungs were burning when another figure darted out from behind a nearby tree.

"No!" she screamed as strong arms reached out and circled her waist.

"Nan! It's me," a familiar voice said into her ear.

"Ned!" Nancy went limp with relief. Turning in his arms, Nancy stared up at his familiar face. "Ned, someone is trying to kill me. We've got to get out of here—he's got a knife."

"A knife? What are we waiting for?"

As they tore to the end of the tree-lined path, Nancy kept glancing back over her shoulder until she was convinced he wasn't following them any longer. Only then did she begin to breathe easily.

"We'll have to report this creep to campus

security." Ned stared deep into Nancy's eyes. For the first time she noticed how handsome he was in his crisp white shirt and charcoal gray suit. "I knew something was wrong as soon as I arrived at your room. Bess said something about a note—and that you were waiting for me in College Woods."

"A note? Bess only said that you'd sent a message." Nancy shook her head slowly. "I should have known that it was a setup, but when she mentioned something about a surprise, I didn't question it."

"Some surprise," Ned said darkly. Pulling Nancy against him, he held her close in a long hug. When he finally let her go, Nancy thought she saw a misty haze in his brown eyes.

They walked in silence the rest of the way to the student center. Bess and Jerry were waiting by the door. Bess had decided on the pink dress, Nancy saw, and Jerry was wearing what was probably his only suit—navy.

"Nancy! Thank goodness you're okay." Bess rushed over and threw her arms around Nancy. "When I found out that Ned hadn't sent that note, I felt awful!"

"Are you okay?" asked Jerry.

"I'm fine," Nancy assured them, smoothing her silk dress, "though I didn't plan to go jogging in this outfit."

Bess gave her a curious look. "What?"

Ned explained. "He was still chasing Nancy when I found her."

"Someone wants me off this case," Nancy added, thinking aloud. "And it looks like he's getting pretty desperate." *So am I,* she added silently. *How am I ever going to crack this before game time?*

A campus security guard was standing inside the entrance to the student center. While Bess and Jerry went in to the dance, Nancy and Ned reported the attack on Nancy.

The security guard took down the details. "We have two cars patrolling the campus tonight. I'm going to radio them with this. They'll be on the lookout for this joker."

"I wish that all this *was* a joke," Nancy whispered to Ned as they went inside to the dance.

"It's not," Ned said gravely. "It's deadly serious. But for tonight, I want you to put the case completely out of your mind and have some fun."

"I'll try," Nancy said with a shaky smile.

The dining hall looked even more elegant than it had late that afternoon. Candles now provided the only lighting. The flickering flames cast a warm glow over the entire room.

As her eyes skimmed over the crowd, Nancy spotted Jerry and Bess twirling on the dance floor.

"What do you think?" Ned asked. "Are you too tired to dance?"

Reaching up, Nancy placed her hands on his broad shoulders. "I'll never be too tired to dance with you, Nickerson."

Everything seems clearer in the light of day, Nancy thought as she took a sip of orange juice at breakfast the next morning. Ned was sitting beside her at a table in the student center, now bare of all the previous night's homecoming decorations. Across the table, Bess and Jerry were splitting their second cranberry muffin.

The dance had been a welcome distraction from the case. But now Nancy was eager to get back to work. She had to find Carrie to see if she had lent her costume to anyone, and she wanted to check with the dean to see if he had any information for her. Glancing at her watch, she saw that it was nearly ten-thirty. The game was at two-thirty. Each second was precious now.

"Hi, everyone." Nancy heard Randy before she saw him come over to their table. He pulled a chair up next to Nancy and straddled it. His eyes were red from lack of sleep.

"You look exhausted!" Bess exclaimed.

"I am," Randy admitted, nervously slipping a hand through his dark hair. "It's ironic.

I skipped the dance so that I'd get a good night's rest. But as it turned out, I was home merely to receive a few more threatening phone calls. Finally I just took my phone off the hook."

"Sounds like our creep had a busy night," Ned commented. "Nancy was chased by some guy wearing the team mascot's costume."

"The wildcat?" Randy asked in disbelief.

"A deadly cat," Jerry added. "This one carried a blade."

"What!" Randy exclaimed. Then he shook his head in disgust. "Unbelievable. I'm sorry that you got dragged into this whole thing."

Nancy shrugged. "It's part of being a detective. Call it an occupational hazard."

"Well, I'm still not giving up," Randy vowed. "That creep kept calling last night, but I just kept telling him no dice. I'm not going to throw this game. I'm going to do my absolute best to win today's game for Emerson."

"And we'll be right behind you," Jerry added. "All the guys on the team want to win this one. You can count on us to give it our best shot."

"Thanks, buddy." Randy stood up and shoved his hands in his pockets. "I'll catch you guys later." He gave them a thumbs-up sign. "Wildcats all the way!"

"Good luck!" Nancy watched as he walked

away. She was about to turn back to her breakfast when something struck her. Quickly glancing back at Randy, her eyes traveled from his jacket, to his jeans, and down to his sneakers.

Purple high-top sneakers! Just like the shoes worn by the knife-wielding mascot!

Chapter

Fifteen

O<small>H, NO!</small>" Nancy gasped as a horrible idea occurred to her. Could Randy have been the one to attack her?

"Nancy, what's wrong?" asked Bess. "You look as if you'd just seen a ghost."

Nancy blinked and turned back to her friends. "Not a ghost, a pair of sneakers. Randy was wearing purple high-top sneakers."

"Oh, yeah. I've got them, too," Jerry volunteered, slinging one foot out from under the table.

Nancy stared in disbelief. "You, too?"

"Everyone on the team has a pair of these babies. A local sportswear shop had them spe-

126

cially made for the football players. I know they're kind of weird, but they gave us purple because of our school colors."

"The mascot who attacked me was wearing purple sneakers," Nancy explained. "That's how I knew it was a guy, because his feet were so big."

"You're kidding!" Bess gasped.

Jerry frowned. "That sort of narrows down your list of suspects, doesn't it?"

"I'm afraid it does," Nancy agreed. "Now I'm convinced that one of the guys on the team is behind this mess."

A heavy silence fell over the table. Finally Jerry broke it.

"It makes me sick to think someone on the team would do all this stuff. But if it's true, he has to be rooted out and punished."

"We'll find him," Nancy assured him, "even though it means investigating twenty or so guys in just a few hours."

"Whoa! I hope you're not counting me," Jerry said, alarmed.

Bess giggled. "You've got a good alibi. You were with me when Nancy was attacked by that mascot!"

With a smile, Nancy said, "It's the other players I need to zero in on—especially Josh."

"But Josh was attacked, too," Ned pointed out.

"True, but that whole incident was suspicious." Nancy told the others her theory that Josh might have staged the attack at the library to direct suspicion away from himself.

"Sounds awfully extreme," Jerry commented.

Nancy nodded. "I've been bothered by that, too. I can't help but think our culprit must have some bigger motive than just jealousy or a vendetta against Randy. Whoever's responsible is risking going to jail for attempted murder. That's a pretty high price to pay just to get back at Emerson, or at Randy."

"I see what you mean," Ned said thoughtfully.

"But we still need evidence and motive that Josh is our man," Nancy said, leaning forward in her chair. "Dean Jarvis is looking into his background, but this situation calls for some emergency measures. Here's my plan—"

"Go, Wildcats, go!"

The cheerleaders shook their purple-and-orange pom-poms in time to the cheer, and the crowd responded with rousing applause. Bundled up in sweaters and jackets, Nancy and Bess were in the stands at the big game. Nancy cheered with the rest of the fans, but her whole body was tense with anticipation.

When the referee blew the whistle, a line of Emerson players ran across the field. The kicker positioned in the center sent the ball flying down toward the end zone, where the Russell team waited.

"That's the kickoff," Nancy whispered to Bess. "Time for us to go."

As they descended the bleachers, Nancy's eyes swept over the crowd. Was someone watching them? But no one seemed to notice as the girls climbed down from the stands, exited the stadium, and headed toward the sports center.

Nancy went over the plan with Bess as they walked. "Remember, I need you to guard the outside door while I'm in the locker room. Jerry says that the coach sometimes sends someone back to the locker room for extra equipment during games. If that happens, try to warn me. Think you can handle that?"

"A big, hulking football player?" Bess laughed. "No problem!"

"In the meantime, Ned should be checking in with Dean Jarvis right about now. Who knows, he might have already come up with some helpful information."

Bess grabbed Nancy's arm as they reached the outside door to the locker room. "Be careful, Nan," she warned.

Nodding, Nancy pulled open the door only far enough for her to slip inside.

She paused just inside the door to make sure the coast was clear. All she could hear was the groan of the boiler echoing against the tiled walls. No one was there.

She crept to the far side of the room and glanced over at the inside door, which led to the rest of the sports center. Jerry had told her that it was unlikely for anyone to come in that way during a game. Since there was no way for Nancy to lock the door, it would have to remain unguarded.

Hurrying across the locker room, Nancy went directly to Coach Mitchell's office, her sneakers squeaking on the tiled floor. Rows of shiny lockers were reflected in the glass of the coach's office.

The office door was locked when Nancy tried it. Pulling her lock-pick kit from the pocket of her jacket, Nancy went to work. Every clink of the metallic tool sounded loud to her ears. She kept glancing nervously toward the outside entrance, but no one appeared.

At last the lock clicked open, and Nancy pulled on the door. Her heart racing, she slipped into the office and went over to the desk. One by one, she searched the drawers. In the bottom of the deepest drawer, wedged between some files, she saw something that caught her eye.

"Bingo!" Nancy whispered, tugging at the black woolen ball and shaking it out. A ski mask! So Josh *had* staged that episode at the library. And Coach Mitchell had helped him by playing the masked attacker.

When Coach Mitchell appeared on the scene right after the attack, no one suspected that he'd been in the library all along. He had probably ripped off the mask, ducked out of sight, then returned to the scene a few minutes later.

Moving away from the desk, Nancy surveyed the rest of the office. There was a file cabinet, a few chairs, a water cooler, and an electric typewriter!

It was right in front of her on the desk. Nancy's palms were sweating as she turned on the typewriter and inserted a piece of paper. First she pushed the CAP button, then typed a few words. She held her breath as she hit the letter *E*.

The bottom of the letter was broken off.

This was it! The threatening notes had been typed on this machine!

Nancy froze as she heard the whoosh of a door—the inside door from the sports center. Then came the steady squeak of sneakers on the tile floor. Someone was coming toward her.

She searched frantically around the office, but she already knew there was no way to get out without the person discovering her. And she was clearly visible through the office's glass paneling.

She was trapped!

Chapter

Sixteen

WITHOUT A MOMENT to spare, Nancy ducked down behind the coach's desk. She could hear the footsteps grow louder as the person approached. She just hoped whoever it was didn't come close enough to see her!

The footsteps stopped, and Nancy heard the person begin to whistle absently.

Maybe it's just a maintenance man, she thought hopefully. As silently as she could, Nancy crept around the desk and over to the side of the office. With her nose to the wall, she inched up enough to peer through the glass partition.

Josh Mitchell was walking down the aisle between two rows of lockers, his back to her. He was wearing jeans, a leather jacket, and purple sneakers. In his hands was a cardboard box.

Of course! Nancy thought to herself. Since Josh was on probation, he wasn't even allowed to sit on the bench with the team. But she was still a little surprised to see him there. If the game was so important to him, why wasn't he outside watching it?

As Nancy watched, Josh placed the box on a bench and gingerly removed the lid. He pushed back the sleeves of his jacket. Then he reached into the box and lifted out a strange object. The jumble of wires and clay seemed odd to Nancy— until she saw the face of a clock attached to it.

Adrenaline surged through her as she realized that Josh was holding a bomb!

Gently he lowered the bomb to the bench. He checked his watch, then worked the hands on the timer. He was probably setting it. How long until the thing exploded?

Turning away from the window, Nancy slid back down to the floor. She had seen enough. It was time to call the police.

She crawled back behind the desk and groped for the phone. When her hands closed on it, she pulled it down and crawled into the knee space beneath the desk.

Quickly she punched in the emergency police number. The phone rang twice, then an officer answered.

"This is Nancy Drew," she said in the barest whisper. "I'm at Emerson College. Someone is setting a bomb in the football team's locker room."

The officer started asking her questions, but Nancy was afraid she'd give herself away if she spoke any longer. "This is an emergency!" she whispered. "Please, send help."

As she replaced the phone in its cradle, she felt something strange above her head. Looking up, she noticed a manila envelope taped to the underside of the desk.

What was that doing there? Why would the coach tape something under his desktop—unless it contained information he didn't want anyone else to find.

Reaching up, she lifted the metal prongs on the envelope and slipped out the contents. The envelope contained only a single sheet of cardboard.

Nancy squinted as she studied the print on the cardboard in the dim light under the desk. The date of each Emerson game was listed in a column on the left. Emerson's opponent for each game was listed in a column in the center of the page. The third column was full of numbers, that could have been final scores for each game.

She shook her head. The chart seemed pretty basic. Why would the coach bother to hide it in a secret place? She was about to slide the chart back into the envelope when the numbers at the bottom of the page caught her eye.

Hey, wait a minute—why were scores filled in for games that hadn't been played yet?

Running her finger down the chart, Nancy checked the listing for that day's game: Emerson versus Russell University. The numbers in the third column read: 6–10.

Nancy's gaze lit on a word printed at the top of the third column: *Spread.* The numbers in that column weren't scores at all—they were point spreads. And point spreads were what people used when they bet on sports games. Emerson was supposed to score between six and ten points in that day's game. This was a betting sheet.

"That's it!" she whispered.

Suddenly it all made sense. The Mitchells needed the Wildcats to lose so that they could make money gambling! Nancy had suspected that there had to be a deeper motive for the attacks on Randy. Now she knew what it was.

The coach was involved in a point-fixing operation. That was why he desperately wanted Randy out of the game, and why he had tried to convince Dean Jarvis to let Josh play. That way, he could make sure that the team finished with a score in the right range.

Then something else occurred to her. That first day, when Randy had brought her and Bess to talk to the coach, he'd been talking on the phone. What was it he'd said? Something about it all being on Sunday's game. She'd assumed he was talking about putting all their energy or hopes into the game. Now she realized he must have been talking about money he was betting.

He'd mentioned some numbers, too. The same ones as were listed for that day's game—6–10.

Nancy stared at the scores for Emerson's first three games, which had already been played. I'd be willing to bet that Emerson's final score in those games fits into the point spreads on this chart, she thought to herself. There was one thing she still didn't understand, though. If Randy *had* agreed to lose the game, the coach still wouldn't win unless he scored within the spread range. She couldn't help wondering how Coach Mitchell had been planning to deal with that.

A noise in the locker room reminded Nancy that she wasn't alone. She had all the evidence she needed against the Mitchells. But she still had to address a more immediate problem.

Would she make it out of the locker room in one piece?

Scooting out from under the desk, she sneaked another peek through the glass partition. Josh was carrying the bomb in his hands. He paused at an open door next to the showers, leaned down, and placed the bomb inside.

That's the boiler room, Nancy recalled. Why is he putting the bomb in there?

Josh stepped back, and Nancy saw that the expression on his face was sad and tortured. In that second she actually felt sorry for Josh. He seemed so unhappy, so confused. For a moment he simply stood there. Then he turned and strode down the dim hallway that led to the locker room's outside door.

Nancy dashed out of the coach's office, then suddenly stopped short. She was no expert on explosives, but she knew enough to wonder whether this bomb could be set off by a sudden movement.

She could hear its timing device counting off the seconds, the sound echoing ominously through the empty room. Tick, tick, tick . . .

Chapter

Seventeen

NANCY GULPED back her fear. She had to find away to get Josh to deactivate that bomb.

"Josh, come back!" she shouted.

She saw him start, then snap his head around to look over his shoulder. The instant his gaze lit on Nancy, he began to run.

He plunged into the dark end of the hallway. There was a flash of daylight as he threw open the door. A moment later Nancy heard him groan as his arms and legs flailed in the air.

Running to the doorway, Nancy saw that Josh was lying prone on the ground. He was hugging his chest and gasping for air. Bess stood over him, her arms folded across her chest.

"I tripped him," she announced proudly. "Are you okay? What happened in there?"

"Plenty," Nancy said, "but I don't have time to explain. We're on a tight deadline." She looked down at Josh. "Aren't we, Josh?"

Josh shook his head, his chest still heaving. "I'm not going back in there. No way."

"I've already called the police," Nancy said. She squatted beside him and looked into his eyes. "You're in enough trouble already, Josh. It'll be a lot worse if that bomb goes off—especially if someone gets hurt."

"A bomb!" Bess gasped. "When is it going to go off?"

"A few minutes before halftime," Josh spat out, "and there's nothing you can do about it."

Nancy wasn't sure exactly how much time they had, but she knew they needed to work fast. "Is there any way to dismantle it?" she asked.

"Of course," Josh replied. He sounded offended. "I made it myself. I know how to take it apart." He looked from Nancy to Bess, a mixture of defiance and fear in his eyes. "But I'm not going to. My old man is really angry at me as it is. I'm not going to ruin this now."

Nancy's palms began to sweat. How was she going to get him to deactivate that bomb? "You seem to know a lot about explosives," she said in what she hoped was an admiring tone.

"I've always been a science whiz," Josh told

her proudly as he climbed to his feet. "People think I'm a dimwit because I'm on probation. It's not true."

"I think you had to be pretty clever to plan all those things designed to hurt Randy Simpson," Nancy said, shooting Josh a dazzling smile. "The fire, the loose weights, the sleeping pills—even the float. You managed to pull them all off without getting caught."

"Some of them were easy," Josh said arrogantly. "With a little kerosene, that platform turned into a tinderbox. People thought Kristin started it with her baton, but that was an illusion. I just had to toss a match from the side of the stage.

"The other things were easy, too," Josh continued. "Carrie never even missed her wildcat costume. She keeps it in a closet near the girls' locker room. It was a cinch to borrow and return it without her knowing. And as for the guys, well—none of them would ever suspect a teammate of rigging the float or drugging a fellow player."

"But I thought those guys were your friends." Bess said indignantly.

Suddenly Josh's face took on the same sad expression Nancy had glimpsed in the locker room. "I don't have any friends," he mumbled. "When your father plunks you down in a new school every year, you don't have time to get attached."

Nancy felt sorry for him, but she couldn't get the ticking bomb out of her mind. If she didn't talk some sense into Josh, they could all be blown to bits.

"Josh, there's no easy way out of this thing. But if you dismantle the bomb, it'll be a start in the right direction. Please don't let anyone else get hurt."

Josh studied the floor. When he spoke, Nancy had to lean close to him in order to hear. "Oh, all right," he mumbled. His shoulders slumped forward as she led the way back into the locker room and opened the door to the boiler room.

"Stand back," he instructed Nancy and Bess. "I know what I'm doing, but you can never be too careful."

From a measured distance the girls watched as Josh cut two wires and removed the clock. "That'll do it," Josh told them.

Nancy let out a long sigh of relief. At last that dreadful ticking had stopped!

She and Bess followed as Josh took the dismantled bomb over to a bench by the lockers and sat down heavily. Nancy couldn't help asking, "Would it really have been worth it, Josh?"

Josh buried his face in his hands. "Dad was afraid you were getting too close. He didn't like the questions you kept asking. That's why we staged that fake attack at the library."

"I don't get it." Bess was confused. "Why do you and your father want the Wildcats to lose?"

"Money," Nancy answered for him.

Josh nodded. "Dad's got a gambling deal going

with a hotshot bookie. When I'm quarterbacking and Dad is calling the plays, we can usually control the score of a game. The point spread is set in advance. I just make sure our team finishes within the predicted spread."

"Gambling!" Bess gasped. "How awful!"

"But when Josh was put on academic probation, it ruined their whole scheme," Nancy pointed out.

"If Randy had agreed to throw the game when Dad made those phone threats," Josh told the girls, "everything would've been fine. But that didn't work, so Dad figured we could hurt him enough to take him off the roster. A third-stringer would never score against Russell's defense." Josh shook his head sadly. "Too bad the guy refused to cave in."

"Maybe you can fill in a blank for me," Nancy said to him. "I saw the point spread your father bet for this game, six to ten. How could he be sure Randy would score in the right range?"

Josh grimaced. "He couldn't. Dad convinced our bookie to change the bet. We were going for just a straight loss."

"I still don't understand why you set that bomb," Bess put in. "What's the use of blowing up an empty locker room?"

Josh clamped his mouth shut. For a second it seemed as if he might bolt, but then he said, "Oh, what's the use. I might as well tell you. The locker room wasn't going to be empty. Dad's going to take Randy out of the game before halftime and send him here to rest up. The bomb was supposed to go off when Randy was in here and the rest of the players were still on the field—at exactly three thirty-five."

"And kill Randy?" Bess was horrified.

"None of the other threats worked," Josh said helplessly. "If Emerson wins today, my father will lose all our savings." He lowered his voice and added, "And more. This bookie has promised to make us pay—in blood."

"An explosion in the locker room will raise a lot of suspicion," Nancy pointed out.

"Not when the bomb is attached to a boiler that's been acting up for months."

Just then the outside door to the locker room opened and Ned rushed in, scowling. "I didn't get anywhere with Dean Jarvis. He insists that he can report only to the police, said something about confidentiality. I told him it was important but—" He broke off as he noticed the dismantled bomb on the bench next to Josh.

"That's okay," Nancy told him. "We've found some answers on our own. And we just stopped Josh from blowing up Randy."

Nancy looked at her watch. "Uh-oh! It's almost three-thirty. Coach Mitchell will be sending Randy in here any second. I have to get outside to make sure the other half of this crime team doesn't slip past us. Bess can fill you in on what's happened."

"Are you sure you don't need a hand?" Ned asked.

"Stay here and keep an eye on Josh until the police get here," Nancy instructed as she backed out the door.

In the stadium, Nancy stood at the front of the bleachers, behind the players' bench. With just over a minute left in the first half, the score was ten to six in favor of Emerson. Way to go, Randy! Nancy thought with a smile.

Nancy checked her watch as the coach called a time-out: 3:31. Just four minutes until the intended explosion time. Coach Mitchell motioned Randy off the field and spoke with him briefly. Nancy wasn't surprised when Randy nodded at the coach, stripped off his helmet, and started jogging down the path toward the locker room.

As Randy passed her, Nancy shivered to think what might have happened to him if she hadn't stopped Josh in time. She waited until Randy had disappeared, then walked onto the edge of the playing field and joined Coach Mitchell.

"Coach," she said firmly, "you're needed in the locker room right away."

Nancy could see a flash of annoyance in his eyes as he peered down at her. "I can't leave the field now! My team is in the middle of play."

"But it's an emergency," Nancy persisted. "It's Josh—I'm afraid he's been hurt."

For a moment the coach froze. He stole a quick

glance up at the clock on the scoreboard, which now read 3:33.

"My son—" Coach Mitchell said in a horrified voice.

Before Nancy could say anything more, the coach turned and tossed his clipboard to the ground. "I have to save him," he mumbled, then scrambled down the path toward the locker room.

Nancy followed as quickly as she could, catching up with the coach just as he threw open the door and bounded inside.

"What!" Coach Mitchell bellowed, skidding to a halt.

Looking over his shoulder, Nancy saw that the police had arrived. A tall, lanky officer was handcuffing Josh.

"Why, you little—" The coach spun around, his face mottled red and purple.

A moment later he lunged at Nancy, his large hands grabbing for her throat.

Chapter

Eighteen

Nancy reared back in shock, and the coach's hands closed over thin air. With lightning speed, she grabbed one of his arms and twisted it behind his back. A moment later the tall officer was clapping a pair of cuffs around Coach Mitchell's wrists.

"*You* did it!" the coach sputtered, glaring at Nancy and struggling against the officer. "You turned these people against me!"

"That's not true," she said, facing him squarely. "You were using the Wildcats—manipulating the team's performance so that you could make money."

The coach let his gaze drop to the floor. "I have nothing to say," he muttered.

"It's too late for that, Dad," Josh said wearily. "She's already guessed everything. It's all over now."

"I've never been so scared in my life!" Bess insisted. "Nancy just pointed at the bomb and told him to defuse it! Can you believe that?"

Ned slipped an arm around Nancy's shoulders and pulled her close. "Sounds pretty exciting to me."

"For the moment I'm just glad it's over," Nancy said, smiling up at him.

She and Ned were sitting on the hood of her Mustang in the parking lot outside the stadium. Alumni and students were gathered in clusters for the traditional post-game tailgate party. Even though Emerson had lost, spirits were high.

"And all this was going on while we were playing the first half?" Jerry asked. "Sounds like the real action was happening off the field."

Bess nodded. "By the time you guys filed in at halftime, the Mitchells had already been taken to the police station."

"Dean Jarvis tells me that charges have been filed against Josh and his father," Ned told Nancy. He rubbed a hand over her shoulder to warm her up. "They're gone now, and I can't say that I'll miss them, even if Josh was a great quarterback."

"But you've still got an honest quarterback on the roster," she said.

Ned followed her gaze to a nearby Jeep, where Randy was digging into a cooler to find sodas for two cheerleaders. "That's true. And it looks like Danielle hasn't tarnished his reputation completely," he added, chuckling.

Nancy laughed. "He really did do a pretty good job in today's game. Even though the Wildcats lost, they scored seventeen points. The Pirates only beat them by three."

"Hey, the dogs are ready." Hopping off the car, he went over to the portable charcoal grill that he and Jerry had set up.

"Good," Bess said, "because I'm famished."

Ned returned with a platter of hot dogs loaded with mustard and onions, and they all dug in.

Nancy had just taken a bite of one when she noticed some familiar faces a few cars over.

"Hi, Nancy," Susannah Carlson called. She looked cute in a pair of tight black jeans and a sweatshirt with *Emerson* emblazoned on the front.

Nancy waved. "Congratulations on the big win," she told Zip. He was wearing jeans and a red sweater. Tamara was clinging to his arm.

"Hey, when I make a promise, I deliver," Zip said with a wide grin.

"We heard about the Mitchells," Tamara told Nancy, "about how you discovered that they were the ones trying to hurt Randy. I don't know how you figured it out. They seemed like clean-cut, all-American football heroes."

"Looks can be deceiving," Nancy pointed out.

"Hey, Susannah," Ned called over from Nancy's Mustang, "nice sweatshirt."

Susannah glanced down at it and blushed. "Oh, I guess you could say that I've come to terms with good old Emerson this weekend. I realized that I'm just bitter because I never got my college diploma. So I've decided to go back to school—in Chicago. And this time I'm going to finish."

"That's great," Nancy told her.

"Well, good luck," Ned said.

"Thank you, Ned." Susannah smiled. "And if you folks ever need any special spices, call me. Susannah's Spices. I'm in the Yellow Pages."

Ned linked his fingers through Nancy's and gave her hand a squeeze. "Thanks, but with Nancy around, life is spicy enough!"

Nancy's next case:

Working as a ski instructor at the posh Tall Pines cross-country resort is a dream job for Nancy's friend George. But ever since Rebecca Montgomery was fired from the resort for stealing, it's been all downhill. George is convinced that Rebecca was set up to take a fall, and she calls in Nancy to pick up the pieces.

Posing as a reporter for a ski magazine, Nancy sets out to uncover the clever culprit behind the cross-country double-cross. But she soon finds how chilling the winter wonderland can be. A soothing sauna turns into a steamy trap; a simple flower holds a sinister secret; and an excursion in the snow leads down a trail of terror . . . in *THE WRONG TRACK*, Case #64 in The Nancy Drew Files™.